ANGELA YURIKO SMITH

Inujini

Contents

Foreword

One of the things I've learned in 7+ years of writing historical fiction is that readers love to find new things about history, particularly history they thought they knew. Because authors can go deep in fiction, we are often able to dig up little known facts and expand on timelines, and in the process show that conventional knowledge is usually only half-true.

This is the case with Angela Yuriko Smith's fascinating first novel.

Inujini tells the story of the Ryukyuans (also known as Shimanchu and Uchinanchu), the indigenous people of Okinawa prefecture in Japan. Today, Okinawa's story is not well known outside of southeast Asia, and particularly for Westerners, for whom Okinawa is mostly known as the scene of the last big battle of WWII and for its ongoing role as a U.S. military base in the Pacific.

The popular narrative is that the war in the Pacific theater was solely between Japan and the U.S. We think of the people on the islands (which are halfway between the southernmost tip of Japan and Taiwan) as Japanese. We're told that 150,000 Japanese civilians were killed in the battle for Okinawa, mostly through coerced suicide when, according to the history books, Japanese authorities encouraged tens of thousands of Okinawans to commit suicide rather than allow themselves to be captured. This, they were assured, would preserve their honor.

I'm half Japanese. My mother was a teenager in Japan during the war. When I was very young, I was foolishly proud of these Japanese who chose death over dishonor. That is precisely the point of such stories. Fairy tales spun about national spirit and identity are meant to promote a sort of rabid nationalism, an unhealthy nationalism. It wasn't until I had studied genocides and mass atrocities as an intelligence analyst that I recognized it for the government propaganda that it is.

In *Inujini*, we learn that Okinawa was primarily peopled not by Japanese but Ryukyuans. That puts a different light on those coerced suicides, the supposed devotion to the emperor. In *Inujini*, we learn that the civilians on Okinawa did not think of themselves as Japanese. The Japanese Army that came to repel the U.S. military were as much invaders as the Yankees. They valued their lives and the lives of their family members more than the Japanese authorities did, obviously. They didn't necessarily want to kill themselves so the emperor, on the brink of defeat, could save face.

Angela Yuriko Smith renders this complex human dilemma beautifully, as she does the terror of being caught in the crossfire of combat. *Inujini* is a story about war, but it not solely about bullets and bloodshed. It's also about resilience of the human spirit, particularly that of girls and young women who, in this time period, tended to have no say in what was expected of them. What was demanded of them.

For that reason alone, *Inujini* can be seen as a must-read tale of war. But Angela Yuriko Smith shows that there is much, much more to the story.

Alma Katsu is the award-winning author of eight novels, including The Fervor, a reimagining of the Japanese internment which was named a best book of 2022 by NPR and Library Journal.

Preface

"Japan first colonized the Ryukyu Kingdom and renamed it Okinawa Prefecture in 1879 through military force in violation of international law including the UN Declaration on the Rights of Indigenous Peoples. Following the annexation, the government of Japan banned the Indigenous language and culture and imposed colonial rule and imperialization policies upon Okinawa, profoundly damaging the unique culture and language of Indigenous Ryukyuans."

From the *Observations on the State of Indigenous Rights in Japan Prepared for United Nations Human Rights Council: 4th Cycle of Universal Periodic Review of Japan 42nd Session of the Human Rights Council*

This story is about the Ryukyuan people (also known as Shimanchu and Uchinanchu) and what they endured during WWII on Okinawa Prefecture. A chain of islands that stretches southwest from Kyushu to Taiwan, formerly known as the Ryukyu Kingdom from 1429 to 1879. The Ryukyu Kingdom was formally annexed and dissolved by Japan in 1879 to form Okinawa Prefecture.

I think my family left Okinawa Prefecture just prior to WWII, but the details have been purposefully lost. When memories are too horrible to relive, they get buried. New memories are planted. Ignorance is a blissful coping mechanism.

"Don't talk about the past or it will return," my Uncle Shigaru told me when I asked.

I'm sorry, Uncle. We didn't talk about it, but the past is returning anyway.

I respect those who choose to forget, but our future depends on remembering.

During the Battle of Okinawa, an estimated 150,000 indigenous Ryukyuans were killed. This was nearly half of the pre-war population of about 300,000. More native islanders died than either of the parties involved: the Japanese and the Americans. Those who suffered the most were not even part of the fight. A name for the island wide devastation was *inujini*, a dog death — an unnecessary cruelty.

Isn't that all war? Whatever we call it, those that have no stake usually suffer the most.

While the United Nations recognizes the Ryukyuan people as indigenous, Japan does not. Japan leases the Ryukyuan land to the US military despite the protests from those who live there. United States military bases on Okinawa Island cover 25% of the land. The bases desecrate burial grounds and destroy the unique ecosystem. Of all the military bases in Japan, 62% are located on Okinawa Island with little financial compensation to the people who live there.

I'm third-generation Ryukyuan, and at 55 years old I'm just discovering this information. Thanks to Meiji-era suppression, much of the islander culture has been erased. I've been told that school and history books are being rewritten to forget atrocities like the military ordered Group Self-Determination (group suicide). Customs were outlawed, such as hajichi, the practice of women tattooing the backs of their hands. The native language has been discouraged and forgotten until they have become classified as endangered languages by UNESCO.

The Ryukyuans, a spiritual, peaceful and egalitarian people, deserve to be heard. Today the Ryukyuan people ask for their land to be returned to them and the US military bases to be removed but they continue to be occupied, discounted and voice-less.

To date, there have been 9,000 murders, rapes and robberies committed by US service members against the indigenous Ryukyuan people. The cases for sexual assault are higher on the military bases located on Okinawa than anywhere else in the world. One of the youngest victims of rape was nine months old. The people objected with the Koza Uprising on December 20, 1970.

Okinawa was claimed by the US after World War II because it was such a strategic location for military bases. The US sold Okinawa back to Japan for six hundred eighty-five million dollars despite protests from the people they were selling.

"Don't talk about the past or it will return," my Uncle Shigaru said.

We have been quiet and it has returned anyway. It's time to be unquiet.

This is an unquiet story.

One

Shigeko, Zamami Island, May 31, 1945

Shigeko hurried by the long line of men that waited for a turn at sex. The sun was barely up, but already at least a hundred men stood in line. Shigeko could smell them as she passed—sweat, tobacco and the cheap cologne meant to cover up the first two odors. She held her breath and walked fast.

The Japanese soldiers had told her she was lucky because the foreign girls in the comfort house kept them happy. At 14, Shigeko didn't know much about sex, but five girls didn't seem enough to service the 1,000 men stationed on her island. It was only a matter of time before they wore out and the soldiers would need new girls.

Just beyond the line of men, she set her eyes on the school door. Often the men yelled at her, asking if she was afraid. Shigeko was, but she couldn't articulate why. It was the way the older women acted that made her afraid. Their economy of movement, lack of eye contact and low voices communicated danger: there were predators near. Some days Shigeko made it past the line without attracting attention. This was not one of those days.

"Little Flower, come keep us company!" The men laughed as a group and started calling her.

She could feel the eyes on her developing curves even though she had taken to wearing trousers and long shirts. Shigeko walked faster, hoping they wouldn't continue their calls. They continued.

"What's the hurry? Do you think I smell bad? You don't like soldier meat?"

A chorus of laughter followed.

"Don't worry, I'll protect you."

Shigeko looked back to see one of the men leave the line. He smiled like a hungry cat. Panicked, she bolted the last few feet into the school.

Her teacher was waiting, holding the curtain back. They were both shaking.

Ms. Toma was pale with shadows around her eyes. "Are you okay? I thought…"

Ms. Toma stopped herself, took a deep breath and smiled brightly. It was thin and false, but Shigeko couldn't blame her. They were all doing their best.

"I'm glad you could make it today, Shigeko."

Only a few older girls still met for school. The soldiers insisted it was important for the teenage girls to continue. The few girls that tried to stay home wound up having soldiers come to their houses to check up on them. Shigeko didn't want more soldiers at her home. Her family already housed two as part of their duty.

"Let's start the day by learning about Himeyuri Gakutotai, the Lily Princesses Student Corps. The students from Daiichi Women's High School and Okinawa Shihan Women's School are forming a nursing corps. These girls will serve an important duty for the Imperial Army. They will have valuable skills when the war is done and be able to work in the medical field anywhere in the world. They will be earning their own money, respect and privileges."

Ms. Toma held up a newspaper with a photo of the Lily Princesses. They looked smart in their uniforms with special badges. All the Princesses wore their hair in braids to keep it neat. Shigeko wanted to be part of the Lily Princess Corps. She imagined returning to her family as a rich woman of the world. Her baby brother would have a pedal car like she had seen in magazines. Her family would move into a beautiful house in Naha.

Shigeko raised her hand. "Can we be part of the Lily Princesses?"

"Yeah, I'll let you practice on me." A man's voice came from beyond the curtained doorway.

Ms. Toma jumped up with a screech. Newspaper pages scattered on the floor around her. The soldier that catcalled Shigeko was in the doorway, grinning. He pulled a rolled cigarette from behind his ear, struck a match and lit up.

"This is a school. Please don't disrupt my students." Ms. Toma sounded stern but Shigeko could hear a tremble in her voice. "Leave now." Ms. Toma pointed her finger past him and out the door.

The soldier exhaled smoke into the room. Shigeko looked away from him, trying to be invisible, but the stink of his tobacco found her.

"I just wanted to ask my Little Flower here why she wouldn't stop and talk. I want her to like me."

"Get out now!" Ms. Toma shrieked.

The soldier turned his attention to her instead.

"Oh, jealous of the attention? Maybe you'd rather talk to me."

He stepped into the classroom and the curtain fell behind him, blocking the outside view. Ms. Toma backed up until her leg touched the little iron stove they used in winter. The scattered news pages tore under her feet as she shuffled. The soldier exhaled again, the cloud of smoke wafting through the room. Shigeko had to do something. It was her fault he had followed here. She put her palms over the lucky shiisaa she always carried with her in her pockets.

Please... please make him leave... please...

Suddenly, a loud blast shook the classroom. It sounded like it came from somewhere beyond the village. They all jumped in their seats and listened for the sirens. The soldier tossed his smoke on the floor and hurried out. As soon as he was gone, Ms. Toma picked the lit cigarette up and threw it in the stove to smolder before moving to the doorway to watch the soldiers from behind the curtain. A few of them shouted to a jeep passing through. She listened, hidden, and then whispered over her shoulder to her students.

"It's okay, the war hasn't reached us yet. It was an accidental grenade. No one was hurt." Ms. Toma gave the same thin, false smile. Her bottom lip trembled.

Shigeko knew no one believed her. It was always okay. No one was ever officially hurt, but they all knew of brothers and fathers that didn't return after one of these accidental grenades. She kept her thoughts away from her own father. Once he had been a caretaker at the advanced school. Now he was out digging for the soldiers. He was at risk for being in an accident. She tried not to think of him. If she didn't think of him perhaps death wouldn't either.

"And I think that's enough school for today, and perhaps tomorrow, too. Gather your things and go home." Ms. Toma waved them away with shaking hands. Class had lasted less than an hour. The building was empty in minutes.

Shigeko left on the other side of the building rather than go straight home. She was too scared to go past the line of men again. It was longer, but she could run around the outside of the village against the sea cliffs. There were soldiers there too but they were always busy digging with island men, or at least yelling at the island men to dig.

The men from her village were sturdy and worked hard, but still the soldiers were never happy. They called them names like *dojin*. Her mother said it meant aboriginals and it was meant as an insult. The soldiers said they were savages. They acted like the islanders were animals.

Shigeko thought this was unfair. When her islands had been the Kingdom they were known as the most hospitable of people by kings. Once her people had their own royalty and castles. Their navigators were sought after by other nations. There was no pleasing the soldiers, though.

On the way home today she saw a group of them hiding a Shinyo, one of the tiny motorboats meant to ward off the American soldiers. She heard there were suicide boats like this hidden around the island. The pilot of each boat would consider it his honor to give his life for his country. When the Americans came, the Japanese would be ready.

As much as Shigeko didn't like the soldiers in her home, they were better than the ones that might soon invade. Officers had come into the classroom a month ago to warn them of all the horrible things the invaders would do to captives. It would be better to participate in what they called Group

Self-Determination they said, rather than let themselves be captured. At first she was confused by what they meant and then the meaning became clear—if the enemy came close enough, the students should kill themselves.

Shigeko stopped to watch the soldiers load the little wooden boat on a cart before rolling it into a shallow cave in the cliff face. The bomb was hidden under a door in the front of the boat. After the craft was safely inside, the soldiers directed the islanders to replant clumps of pampas grass across the cliff to hide the entrance. Someone was walking up behind Shigeko and she turned to see one of the soldiers. He smiled.

"Candy?" he asked. He held out a small paper sack to her. He shook it like she was a hungry dog. She shook her head and bolted, terrified at the attention. Her feet pounded along the beach spraying sand behind her. She wondered how many more times she would be running from these men before they returned to their own homes.

None of them felt like giving chase to an agile native girl. Their stiff leather boots were not suited for the sand. They struggled to march once they were off the wide, stone roads that crossed the island. Shigeko ran through a wild field of grass full of giant stalks that would hide her. She didn't stop running until she burst into her own house.

"Shigeko!"

She startled her mother and little brother, Chiga, who started crying. Mother soothed him, rubbing his back. To calm him, Shigeko poured the last dribbles of tea from a jar for him to drink. He hiccuped into the cup, blowing bubbles from his nose.

"What is it, Shigeko? What could cause you to fly in here like that?"

Mother sounded superficial, like they were play-acting, but her eyes were full of fear.

"Soldiers scared me," Shigeko said. "I over reacted." She was calm now, not wanting to frighten Chiga again. Her mother reached around and started inspecting Shigeko, tugging on her clothes. Chiga was almost tipped from her lap.

"Did they touch you?"

"No. I was just scared. They wanted to give me candy."

"Shigeko, you know better than to get near the soldiers. Never let them get close enough to…"

Mother trailed off, but Shigeko knew what happened when you got too close to soldiers sometimes. They had their foreign girls in their pleasure house, but there were rumors that not all the soldiers liked to stand in line.

"I know, Mother. I ran. I didn't let them get close and I ran."

Her mother pulled her close, squeezing her in a half hug around Chiga, and kissed her head. The little boy protested at being squeezed between the women in his life.

"Did you bring me candy, Shigeko?" he asked from between them.

"Chiga, everyone knows candy from soldiers is dirty. They keep it in their sweaty boots where it starts to stink."

"Ew!" That was too much for Chiga. He squeezed from between them and crawled away to play with the tiny clay animals their grandmother had made them. Originally made for Shigeko, the animal collection had passed to Chiga. Shigeko kept two of the figurines as treasures from Babaan—the set of lucky shiisaa in her pockets. Chiga coveted the guardian lion dogs, but Shigeko wasn't ready to pass them on forever. Still, she let him watch them sometimes.

Her mother was slicing potatoes for their soup. Soon the soldiers that lived with them would return along with her father. For the few moments they had until then, the house felt like it was theirs. Shigeko didn't think about the explosion. She pushed the soldier and his candy from her mind. There were only so many worries one could bear, and for now she would rest from all of them. She took her shiisaa from Chiga, slipped them back in her pockets and went to help mother chop vegetables.

When her father did return she hugged him and tried not to look upset, but he understood. He would have heard the explosion too. He knew his family would be worried, wondering if he was coming home. He knew men, friends of his, that hadn't.

Then the soldiers that stayed with them returned, and Shigeko's family became polite like strangers.

Two

Yuki, South Okinawa, Night Visitors

The headache was back.

Yuki pulled the sheet over her head to block out the world. Even the scratch of her skin against the bedding was too loud. The quiet village she called home was a cacophony of shrill sound. Besides the loss of vision, her tongue and fingers were numb. The pain behind her right eye was so intense she thought she might vomit in the bed. The headaches started up a few months ago and no one seemed surprised. Her mother said she was being called with no other explanation. She called it kami-daari. Yuki worried that she might be stuck with the headaches forever.

The barrage of explosions to the South added to the suffering. Her father said the enemy was just off shore in massive ships firing at the beaches. No one knew why. The Ryukyuan people had done nothing, had no enemies. Their only crime was being under Japanese rule. She heard whispers from the elders… perhaps they should not have allowed the Japanese such an easy claim. Let the Japanese think what they want, they said at the time. It didn't matter what these bossy strangers thought… until now.

Yuki squeezed the two little clay shiisaa in her fists. Her mother had made them for her when she had been young, and they were her best friends. Round like balls, Mama had poked little faces into the clay and scratched curly manes and happy, smiling eyes into the red mud. Shiisaa were protective guardians, Mama told her. Keep them with you and they will bring you luck and protection.

Yuki always carried them—the male in her right pocket to scare away bad luck and spirits and inhale the good. The female was always in her left pocket to seal out bad luck and spirits and seal in the good. Babaan, her grandmother, said together they made the sound Aum. 'A'() from the male and "fiūṃ" () from the female. Each doing an equal part, together the sang "Aum" (ॐ) which was the sound of absolute balance and harmony.

So many nights Yuki fell asleep listening to their soothing song in her dreams. Though she was almost a woman now, she still talked to them and they still answered back. Even now with the blinding headache and the attack of their island, the shiisaa gave her comfort. Eventually the pain subsided as the calming song played through her mind and Yuki fell asleep.

She woke up with the pain subsided, but to silence. The distant explosions had paused, but that wasn't the silence that unnerved her. Yuki had lived in this house her entire life and she was familiar with every creak and sigh of the structure and the occupants. Her mother's soft, whistled breathing. Her father's throaty snore. The comforting sounds of sleeping were absent and the small room felt huge and empty. Only a small warmth at her back let her know she wasn't completely alone.

"Shoji?"

She whispered into the dark. Her little brother was usually spooned up next to her. She could tell he was wide awake, sitting upright in the bed. He didn't answer. She often called him a chatterbox and wished he would give her some quiet. This silence was worse. She turned in the bedding, twisting her head to find him in the dark. She sensed him there, staring at the front door, though she could barely see anything. Her skin chilled into tiny bumps. She whispered again, softer.

"Shoji? What's wrong?"

Again, no answer. She would have thought he was asleep but for the tension running through his small body. She started sliding out of the bedding to sit up when his small hand came out of the dark and touched her face. Yuki stopped moving.

"Mama's gone."

Shoji's voice was rough and thick like he'd been crying. This wasn't upsetting on its own. In Yuki's mind, he was always crying when he wasn't chattering, but this silence wasn't like him. Her baby brother was scaring her along with the empty room and the eerie lack of explosions. Being scared brought out the worst in Yuki. She pushed him away roughly and sat up.

"Mama is not gone, you baby. They are just gathering extra wood and grass in case we don't want to leave our house."

This was somewhat true. It was the answer all the parents were giving when they told the children to stay inside instead of doing their chores. As nice as it was to get out of working, none of the younger children were enjoying it. The air shimmered with barely transparent fear.

"But that was our job. Why do they want our job?"

"They don't want our jobs." Yuki snapped at him. In truth, she was also scared but she had to hide it for Shoji. Her baby brother started making the breathy hiccup noises he always did before he started crying. That was the last thing she wanted right now. Her nerves were already pulled tight and she needed a minute to think.

"What was that? Did I just hear Mama?"

She forced her voice to take on a playful tone and it worked. Shoji brightened up.

"Mama?"

His voice was soft and hopeful. It reminded her of how much of a tender baby he still was. Barely five, he still depended on their parents for so much. She was almost an adult. She knew she should be kinder to him.

"Yes, I thought I heard her. Didn't you? Let's listen."

They both became still in the dark, listening.

"I don't hear…"

Yuki clapped her hand over his mouth. She had actually heard something, but it wasn't their parents. Someone was walking in the clearing outside but the footfalls were heavy and hard. They were solid, like pony hooves in the dirt. Whoever was walking outside their house was clumsy. They kicked small stones that sounded as loud in the silence as any of the bombs the enemy had fired at them that day.

She imagined the whole village huddled inside their houses, listening. Surely some of the fathers would come out to investigate this intruder. Then she had a chilling thought: what if they were alone? What if everyone in the village had somehow left them behind? She needed to peek out through the crack in the door. Yuki started to get up silently but Shoji clutched at her. She could tell he was shaking his head in the dark.

"Don't go…"

It was more a breath than actually speaking. His tiny hands were so strong when he was scared. She'd experienced this once when she had swam out to rescue him from a strong current. Instead of clinging to her back as she'd expected, he panicked and nearly drowned them both as he clawed her face trying to escape the sea. He had been so terrified she couldn't pull him off. His body was as tense now as that day. She had an idea.

She found his hands and touched his sweaty palm with her thumb, forefinger and pinky. Instantly she felt the frenetic tension ease from his body. Still, he didn't move so she repeated the movements. Even though she couldn't see him, she knew he had cocked his head in the dark. She had caught his attention.

"Buu saa shi…" she whispered.

He was still for a few seconds, considering if his big sister was trying to play a joke on him, and then he nodded. There were few things Shoji liked more than playing buusaa.

Yuki nodded to let him know they would begin. They touched hands so they could feel if the other tried to cheat. Together, they swung their hands down three times and each thrust out a digit. Both had chosen buu, the thumb. This was a draw. They had to play again. He gave a tiny giggle in the dark. Yuki indicated they would try again.

Together, they repeated their movements. This time, Yuki won. Predictably, Shoji chose his thumb again. He almost always chose his thumb. Yuki chose shi, her pinky. Shi beats buu. Her little brother huffed his disappointment. Yuki shrugged and started sliding out of the bed. Shoji tried to hold her back but she poked her pinky into his palm to remind him. She had won and now he had to honor that. Reluctantly, he let go.

Silent, she crept across the packed dirt floor and looked out of the crack that also served as a peep hole. A sliver of her village came into view. Not much to see except the corner of a house, the view alongside it and a few fence posts.

The hard earth that served as a gathering place was cast in shadow with the moon not yet out. She was conscious of how loud her breath sounded against the door as she strained to see more from her limited vantage point. At the edge of her vision was the large banyan tree that spread wide over many of the houses on this end. During the day it created a cool refuge. Tonight it felt less friendly, sheltering hidden threats in the shadows. Yuki thought she saw a movement and she pressed her face into the wood, trying to see.

Suddenly the back door creaked open. Shoji, silent all this time, shrieked. Yuki whipped around, completely surprised by the sudden movement behind her and also screamed. She hadn't thought to check the back entrance, and now it was too late. Whatever she had been looking for out there was now in here. In a panic, she slid down the door, still screaming. The dark figures rushed through the back door and straight to the bed to grab her brother. Yuki found a sandal on the floor next to her and hurled it across the room at the attacker. It hit, but the shoe was too light to do much damage.

"Hey! Calm down both of you!"

The other figure dropped bundles to the floor and groped and banged until suddenly the lamp flared up and there was light. Her mother was kneeling over the now hysterical Shoji, struggling to calm him down. Her father stood surrounded by dropped bundles of driftwood and sticks. Fresh sea grass was piled up as well. He hissed at them, his authority overriding the children's terror.

"Hush, both of you! It's only us! We expected you to be asleep by now!"

Shoji had calmed to a whimper, face buried in Mama's arm. Yuki was so relieved she jumped up and ran to her father, grateful even for his gruff scolding. She wrapped her arms around his waist as he put the lamp back out to save fuel, set it down and then embraced his daughter.

"Why are you two still awake?" he asked. His voice was low, signaling to the children to keep their voices low as well.

Yuki had her own face buried in the stiff fabric of her father's summer kimono so her whisper was muffled but audible.

"We heard a noise. I thought it was the enemy because the bombing stopped."

A sudden urge to cry took over Yuki but she resisted. She had to set a brave example for Shoji but the tears squeezed out anyway. Her father bent over her and kissed the top of her head. That was enough and Yuki was overtaken by quiet sobs. The headache, the constant threat of invasion and now the eerie silence which was somehow worse… all of it came together in a wave to unhinge her resolve.

The parents made no move to calm their children but just held them tight. There were no explanations. Mother crooned to Shoji from the bed and the little boy's sobs soon quieted into light snores. As for Yuki, she only allowed herself a few minutes of tears before she regained control. She was older, and nearly an adult. Tears were for children. Still, she clung to her father until she became sleepy, too. Whatever had been outside didn't matter. Her parents were home and now they were protected. Nothing would dare come into their small house now.

Yuki's father guided her to bed where Mother was tucking in her brother. She was grateful to snuggle next to him. Her parents, tired from their own adventures, quickly got ready for bed on their own. Drifting in and out of sleep, the last sounds Yuki was aware of were the familiar breathing of her family, the noise of the cicadas outside and the whispering of the trees around them.

Three

Kaori, North Okinawa, Shiisaa Sighting

"Get on this boat!"

If she hadn't been clutching a newborn baby, Kaori's mother would have jumped out of the boat and wrestled her crazy daughter into their rickety little skiff. She would have tied her up if needed, gagged her to muffle the tantrum screams. In the distance, they could all hear the explosions.

"Kaori! Please! We have to go!"

Kaori backed away another step. She wanted to run through the outgoing tide and join her family. She was terrified of the soldiers that would soon over run everything. She felt too young to be alone, but there was no way she could leave the island, the grove and grotto specifically. Her spirit voice told her to stay, so she would.

The tide was leaving, and with it Kaori's family. Her father was resigned to the loss. Kaori could see it in his eyes. He was sealing her off in his heart, turning his gaze away so as to not see her. It hurt, but she understood. He was practiced at losing things—a first wife and family. A son, her little brother.

"You won't find him."

Her mother's words traveled across the surf to lodge in Kaori's eyes, making them sting. She wanted to ask them to wait. She knew they would. Her father would be relieved, her mother would sob into Kaori's hair. Her baby sister would know her. She swallowed the words back. She had to stay. They were already leaving, going out with the tide.

"I don't know if I want to find him!" Kaori yelled to be heard. "But I still have to stay."

Her mother looked confused and then she too resigned. She was losing another child. Her eyes reflected the pain and then she closed them, sealing it away. Her tears escaped to baptize the new baby.

Kaori could hear gunfire. There were dangerous smells in the breeze. Iron tainted smoke, burning poisons—the smell of strangers. She turned her back on her family and the sea. There was no point in watching the little boat recede into what was now her past. The present moment was calling her attention now. Above the trees there was smoke. The soldiers were here.

There was no time to berate herself for not acting faster. There was no time to wish her family had spent less time preparing to leave and more time leaving. With soldier voices bouncing through the underbrush, there was no way she would be able to get home to hide. Kaori scanned the beach, looking for a miracle.

"Please, show me what to do."

Her words were directed to her spirit voice. Kaori didn't know many things, but she knew to trust this inner voice. Her grandmother had heard it all her life and it had never steered her wrong. Sometimes Kaori felt her grandmother's presence adding volume, texture and depth to what had just been a nudge in her mind before. It was toward this presence she now directed her plea.

"I listened. I stayed. Now please tell me what to do."

For a second out of time, the world paused. Kaori felt the danger waiting. The smoke in the treeline stilled, the unfamiliar yells froze in foreign throats. Kaori felt her mind go flat and smooth like the sand before it expanded to encompass her surroundings. Then she saw it.

At the edge of the treeline, half in shadow, a rocky outcropping peeking out from beneath rotting trunks. Several trees had collapsed, giving their lives in a past typhoon to make this shelter for Kaori now. She sprinted across the sand, racing toward the danger to dive into the tangled pile of deadwood.

Burrowing through the vine and undergrowth, she scrambled to the base of the rocky pile and found a shallow den. It was just big enough for a skinny adolescent girl to slip into, more a hollow beneath the rocks than a cave, but it was enough. Kaori wriggled her way in, her last glimpse of the beach was of the wind wiping the sand clean of her footprints. When she was as far as she could go she closed her eyes and prayed.

She called to her little brother, like her, somewhere still on the island. She was sure he could hear the helicopters and smell the acrid odors they left. Wherever he was, she tried to send her protection. *Stay hidden*, she thought to him. *Don't let them see you.*

She pictured her mother and father in the tiny boat not meant to go too far beyond the coves. It would be in the wide ocean now. If it flipped in the swells her mother and father would be able to paddle themselves to safety, but her baby sister would be lost. Kaori sent breathless whispers of prayer to find them. Then she heard harsh foreign voices yelling words she couldn't understand. She stilled her breath, closed her eyes, willing herself to be a shadow and nothing more.

The shouting and sound of soldiers lasted most of the afternoon. At one point there was gunfire followed by yelling and laughter. Kaori only heard the voices of men but they were nothing like she had heard before. The men she had known all her life had soft, firm voices that blended with the island topography. Their words curved against the sand, wove through the trees and bounced off the waves like song.

The voices she could hear echoing through the trees now jarred her. They fought against the landscape. She could feel the spirits of the island flinching against the discordant dialect with no music in it. Flat, the strange words slapped against the sand like dead fish. The land was shocked but not submissive. It resisted, pushing back against these strangers that didn't belong.

Eventually, the voices faded. It took much longer for Kaori's heart to stop pounding against her ribs, beating her lungs to be free. She lay still in the ensuing quiet. It was too quiet. The animals had fled. No birdsong broke the hush, even the waves seemed to be muted. All lay silent in the humid afternoon, listening with Kaori until eventually she fell into a restless sleep.

She opened her eyes to darkness. There were still no sounds around her except the waves lapping onto the beach. Kaori's stomach was empty but her bladder was full. She wriggled out of her hiding spot and crawled out onto the sand. In a rush, she steadied herself against the trunk and squatted so she could relieve herself, sighing.

The sound of urine hitting the ground echoed from her right. She looked over to see one of the soldiers looking right at her. He had just finished urinating himself and was still exposed. Kaori jumped up, still midstream and tried to dart away but her baggy pants were down. They wrapped around her ankles and she tripped. Bigger and faster, the soldier lunged forward and grabbed her.

Kaori kicked at him but he flipped her around easily so her legs flailed uselessly in the air. She tried to scratch his face but she couldn't reach him from her current angle. She drove her free elbow back, hard and connected with his torso. He grunted and slapped her across her temple hard enough to disorient her. She couldn't understand what the soldier was saying, but his meaning was clear.

He was dragging her back into the trees when he stopped. He was speaking to someone else. She craned her neck to see another soldier. The other soldier pointed at her, shaking his head. They were arguing and Kaori seized upon the chance to drive her elbow back again as hard as she could. She connected with bone and was rewarded with a pained grunt from her captor. Kaori shrieked at him in terror and rage. Her captor slammed her into one of the dead trunks that had sheltered her earlier. She collapsed, her vision disintegrating into starry grains of sand. Kaori was vaguely aware the two soldiers were now yelling over her.

A rush filled her ears. It sounded like the surf had risen in a storm. The soldier that had been leaning on her was suddenly knocked away hard enough that Kaori too was spun around. She lay on her back, disoriented, stunned, staring at the dark canopy. A thick liquid sprayed through the air, cutting across her vision. She struggled to prop herself up on her elbows. Her eyes felt too loose in her head, like they might roll out on their own.

The soldier that had attacked her dangled in the air. He looked like he was being eaten by a lion, half crushed between teeth the size of boulders. He kicked at the monster as helplessly as Kaori had kicked at him minutes earlier. One of his arms was torn off at the elbow, the broken bone jutting from shredded flesh. Blood sprayed everything, including Kaori and the other soldier.

A thick paw came out of the shadows, sinking claws into his torso, piercing the skin to release his innards. Pulling free, a handful of entrails dangled like a nightmare sea creature. The soldier's screams turned into a gargle. The creature dropped the body and turned to Kaori, towering over her.

She was too stunned to move, too terrified to scream, but the beast didn't advance. It growled, extending paws to her as if to embrace. Just behind the tree Kaori could see the other soldier, a red spray of blood across his face in the starlight, but otherwise he was the color of milk.

"Help me, please," Kaori called to him. Her voice trembled with hysteria. The soldier didn't respond. His eyes were fixated on the beast.

The giant animal did respond. It dropped its massive paws back to the ground and went silent, watching her. It was a face she recognized, but her mind refused to make sense of what she was seeing. A curly mane, shining like copper even in the twilight, coal black eyes shining at her from above a gaping grin. It was a shiisaa.

Flat, angry voices tore through the dark. Lights flashed and bobbed through the trees and machine gun fire rang out. The staccato sounds spurred her to action. Kaori backpedaled away from the shiisaa, the soldiers and the gore to scramble, crab-like, across the sand. When she thought she was out of the shiisaa's reach she flipped over and scrambled to her feet, sprinting toward the water.

She charged into the gentle waves waist deep before she risked a look behind her. Neither the remaining soldier or the shiisaa-monster followed. The beach was clear. In the dark edge of the tree line Kaori could see lights darting around, the silhouettes of men flashing in and out. There was more yelling and then the lights and noise converged to a single group.

Beams of light reached across the sand, groping for her. Kaori dove and swam away sideways across the pull of the receding tide as fast as she could. When she surfaced, there was a good distance between her and the chaos she had left. She bobbed in the dark water, watching until she was sure none of them were coming after her and then she swam away.

Kaori had spent her whole life on the island, but she had never spent much time out alone at night this far from their small house. She was disoriented. There was no moon out, both a blessing and a curse. With no moonlight she couldn't be easily seen, but neither could she easily see. The shoreline was a blot of shadow once she was out of view of the soldiers' lights. Still, she felt far from safe. Every patch of dark seemed to be shiisaa shaped and moving. Finally, she swam back to a bare scoop of beach with a flat, grassy expanse of beach grass.

Kaori was hungry and cold. Her long baggy shirt flapped against her as she moved, but she didn't feel comfortable taking it off. The forest was watching her. In the distance she could hear the voices of soldiers still yelling, but she had no way of knowing how many there were. Was that all of them, or were they spread out across the entire island, silent and waiting for a young girl to show up? Now she didn't even have pants to cover herself.

With her bare hands, Kaori dug out a shallow hole in the sand. She pulled the still-warm island back over herself. She lay sideways, back to the sea, watching the trees. If anything came from the treeline, she could sprint for the ocean and be gone fast enough. Certain she would never sleep again, she lay wide awake under the stars in her sand cocoon. The weight of the sand was soothing. Kaori watched the moon rise, her mind blank with shock.

Four

Shigeko, Zamami Island, Birthday Surprise

The next morning Shigeko woke to her mother shaking her awake and sirens.

"The Americans are here!"

Shigeko had never seen her mother so terrified. She scrambled out of bed wide awake.

"The soldiers will protect us?" Shigeko glanced at the side area where the two Japanese assigned to their "hospitality" usually slept. They were hurrying away, strapping on parts of their uniforms as they ran. It was a query rather than a statement.

Her mother spat out the door as they ran.

"Soldiers protect soldiers. They eat our food, steal our men and bring us war. The best thing they could offer us is their absence."

"Do we run to the shelters?" Shigeko's mind was blank. In the weeks leading up to this moment they had all talked about what they would bring and how they would defend their families from the invaders if needed. Now she couldn't think of a single thing to take. In the early morning light, every stick and rag in her house looked precious.

"No, the soldiers said we wait. They will let us know when it is time. They said they will fight the Americans off." Her mother didn't look convinced.

19

They stood together, stunned. Shigeko's mother wrapped her in an embrace. A sleepy Chiga scrambled himself free from the beds and worked his way between them. Shigeko's father came from outside where he had been speaking with the neighbors, all of them trying to piece together what the sirens might mean and what should be done.

"Don't worry, Family. This is just a test." He looked worried though. Her mother broke the moment up with brisk efficiency.

"A test? Why do they bother to wake us up for nothing? We don't need a test, we need them all to leave." She was trying to make a joke but no one laughed. "But we still need breakfast," she said. "Chiga, bring in some wood. Shigeko, start the stove."

They all sprang into action, grateful for something to do. Shigeko ran outside to pull a bucket of fresh water and use the outhouse, while Chiga brought in the kindling and driftwood to fuel their small stove. As she left, it was her brother's turn to use the facilities. She replaced him with the chores, lighting the stove. The wailing of sirens stopped.

Except for waking to sirens, it might be any morning where they were rushing about. Shigeko filled the kettle for tea, and a large, flat pan she oiled with fat. Her mother came in from the garden with a squash and some greens. She watched Shigeko for a moment, and then set the vegetables down.

"We will have an early birthday celebration."

Shigeko would be 15 in three days.

"Now?"

Her mother nodded.

"And I have a special surprise for this special day. You chop these vegetables and I will be back. Leave room in the pan."

Things hadn't been normal for a while and a celebration felt out of place, especially this early. In spite of this, Shigeko felt a shiver of anticipation.

Chiga came in from the outhouse and Shigeko gave him the news.

"We are celebrating my birthday early. Mother went out to retrieve a surprise."

"Ew!"

"What, why is that bad? I'll be fifteen in a few days anyway."

Chiga scrunched his face and whispered.

"Whatever the surprise is, she hid it in the outhouse."

Shigeko didn't know what kind of present would be hidden in the outhouse, or if her little brother was just teasing her. Sure enough, she peeked out the back door just in time to see her mother coming out of the outhouse as she tucked something into the front of her work smock. Shigeko wasn't sure if she wanted this gift after all.

When Mama came in Shigeko and Chiga stared at her, waiting for the surprise to be revealed. She glanced at them without a word and then began setting up for breakfast. After a few seconds she glanced up at her children, trying to suppress a smile.

"What? You have never been to the outhouse before?"

"Yes! But not for a present!" Chiga squealed with laughter, everything else forgotten.

"What? You leave presents in there all the time. I smell them. You don't fool me."

"I don't want one of those presents, if that's what it is!" Shigeko couldn't guess what present would survive being hidden in a smelly place like that.

Her mother slid her hand inside her smock. "Oh, so disappointing. I guess I will keep it for myself."

"Mother!" Chiga ran at her, giggling, and trying to reach in her pocket. "What is it? Is it birthday poop?"

They were all laughing now.

"Yes," said Shigeko's mother. "That's exactly what I have here. Birthday poop… for breakfast!" She pulled a tin of meat out of her pocket and held it up.

"Canned Spam!" shrieked Chiga. "I love Spam in a can!"

"Too bad it's all for me. My birthday, my Spam."

Chiga looked so crestfallen Shigeko didn't have the heart to tease him more like she normally would.

"Of course I'm sharing. You are so gullible. You'll believe anything."

Chiga stopped pouting. "Can I have the key?"

Shigeko's mother had already detached the key from the bottom of the can and was twisting it along the side, coiling the strip of tin neatly. She pulled it away when Chiga tried to touch it. "It's Shigeko's gift, she can decide."

Shigeko had a small collection of these keys already. Decorated with thread, shells and beads, they were something to collect and trade with her friends. The tiny keys were also good as tools. They could be used to shape clay, gouge wood and as a tiny screwdriver. The tiny, metal key that came with each can of meat was as valuable as the contents. If she gave it up, this would be Chiga's first. Spam keys seemed trivial in light of a war looming over them and strange soldiers sleeping in their house.

Shigeko nodded. Chiga started dancing around the small house as their mother cut the little loaf of meat into slices and carefully placed them on the hot pan.

"Shigeko has to uncoil the key from the can though, Chiga. We don't need any cut fingers. Not today."

Her voice had been light until the last two words. Their mother's voice cracked a little, dropped in pitch and left a shadow in the room. As if summoned, their father bustled in making no pretense of the situation. He looked alarmed at the frying meat, raising his eyebrows at Mama with an unspoken question.

"I decided we should celebrate Shigeko's birthday a few days early," Mother said. She turned the sizzling rectangles over with her long chopsticks so they could brown on the other side. The smell filled the room with a savory aroma that caused saliva to flood Shigeko's mouth. Her father looked concerned, glanced at his children and faked a smile. Shigeko was seeing a lot of this type of smile lately.

"Of course! It is always a good time to celebrate something so important!" He stood still in the house, shifting his weight from foot to foot and then turned back to his wife. "Come help me in the garden after we eat. Shigeko can stay home from school today. For her birthday."

Mama stopped poking at the slices of meat and looked up at her husband. She studied him in silence, trying to determine how grim his news was and then nodded. No more words passed between them. Shigeko knew this was going to be a private conversation between her parents. Living in such close quarters, her family had few secrets. Shigeko focused back on carefully unwinding the key from the thin strip of sharp metal on the Spam can.

"Chiga, after we clean up I can show you all the keys I have and help you decorate yours if you want."

Chiga shook his head no.

"I want to keep mine as a key so it can unlock a chest of treasure."

Her little brother was completely occupied in watching Shigeko liberate the key. She glanced up to see her mother smiling gratefully at her. Shigeko shrugged. She was almost a young woman and would have her own children to entertain someday. Her brother was good practice.

"Where are you going to find a treasure chest?" she asked Chiga. He had such a big imagination she was never sure what he was going to come up with.

"From an American soldier of course. When I kill one."

Just then, the key slipped free but Shigeko pulled too hard and was rewarded for her efforts with a thin cut along the tip of her thumb. She winced but didn't cry out. A dark cloud settled over them. The sizzling meat that was making her stomach growl seconds earlier now smelled too potent. Shigeko handed Chiga the key and plastered a fake smile of her own across her face. She wondered if it was part of growing up.

Chiga hugged her and ran out the door to dig roads in the sand with his new possession. Shigeko watched him go as she put her cut thumb into her mouth. She tasted blood and hoped it wasn't an omen of things to come.

The meal was delicious, but she barely tasted it. The slices of crisped meat seemed bland on the tongue but over powering in the nose. Thoughts came to her unbidden, threatening to coax tears from the back of her eyes. Shigeko couldn't cry. That would set Chiga off and no one would have any peace. As a near adult, she wanted to follow her parents into the garden after breakfast to find out what news her father had. Instead, she knew she would be washing up with her brother. She looked at her mother, hoping for intervention. None came.

The conversation was as false as all the recent smiles. They commented on the meal and wished Shigeko a pleasant birthday, but no one said anything of substance. They talked around the obvious without touching it. No one remarked on the sound of blasts in the distance or the groups of soldiers that ran by. There were still slices of crispy meat remaining once the meal was done, unusual for such a treat.

Shigeko's parents hadn't been outside long when a Japanese soldier showed up at the open doorway. He didn't bother introducing himself, just looked at Shigeko expectantly. Without a word she ran to the back and called her parents in. They were sitting on a low fence at the rear of the yard. Mama was crying, her face buried against her father's shoulder. He got up silently and left his wife shaking with sobs on her own. Without a word he followed the soldier outside to the front of the house. Mama came back in from the back smiling, but it did not shine in her eyes like it normally did. They were red and puffy. Even Chiga sensed something was wrong. Her father came back inside as a different man. His tan skin had a tint of ash to it.

"Everyone is meeting at the monument. The entire island. We are supposed to head there now."

"For what?" Shigeko's mother asked. She looked like she might start crying again.

Her father looked over them as if blind. Shigeko was sure she saw tears in the corners of his eyes.

"For insurances." He would say nothing further.

Five

Yuki, South Okinawa, Too Close to Home

When Yuki next opened her eyes, it was to the thin, gray light of morning. Shoji was curled beside her, his toes curled up in the space behind her knees. She could smell his sweet baby breath. Next to her, on the floor, were her shiisaa. There were no booming noises to shatter the island peace. The enemy must have moved on, meaning so could Yuki.

She sat up. A few feet away her parents were still sleeping, exhausted from their late night out. Near the back door were still all the bundles of sea grass her father had dropped. As quietly as she could, Yuki slipped out of bed, kissed each of her shiisaa before pocketing them and pulled a dress over her shorts and tank top.

She started quietly moving the animal fodder outside where it belonged, tidying the mess before her family awoke. She had a buoyant feeling, as if it was a holiday. And wasn't it? Between the absence of her headache and the explosions, everything was back to normal.

Carefully, Yuki picked up all the wood and stacked it next to the small stove. She worked in silence so as not to wake the family, but also to enjoy this time alone. It was a kindness paid to herself as well. The potatoes she picked up and put in the basket, the newer ones behind the older so they would last longer. Then she went outside to take care of the animals, opening the door slowly so as to not make a disturbance.

Outside, the morning was cool and bright. The salty air blew in from the ocean, and it was early enough in the day to still carry the lingering scent of the Sagari-bana that only bloomed at night. Yuki paused to savor the peace, expressing gratitude for the space she enjoyed.

The animals were excited for the early meal. Normally she wouldn't be setting out to gather their fodder for a few hours, Shoji in tow. He annoyed her with his constant chatter and games, but after the terror of the night before she was sure she would be patient with him today.

A feeling pricked at her heart, a discomfort. *Hide, hide!* These words pressed against the inside of her mind. She was being urged to run, but to where? Yuki scanned the trees, the huddle of nearby houses… there was no sign of danger. The entire village was sleeping in. She suddenly felt exposed and alone.

Like the night before, her skin chilled into small bumps. The morning was still bright, but the golden hue leached from the sky. The day felt washed out and flat. The cicadas stopped chittering. Even the breeze paused as if the ocean was holding its breath. A strange odor wafted in the breeze, a metallic burnt smell. A shrill whistle sliced overhead like a razor cutting the wind. The animals deserted their meal and bleated in panic. Confused and afraid, Yuki craned her neck, seeking the source of the sound. Then a plume of earth and splintered forest shot up into the air just outside the village.

She saw it over the trees, a dark jet of soil exploding into the sky as if the earth had turned to water. Clods of earth rained down on the red tile roofs like hail. It was a monsoon of mud. The boom hit a second later and knocked her off her feet. She landed on her backside, hard. Yuki was jarred and disoriented. Her ears were filled with a ringing that muffled the noise of the animals crying out. Someone was screaming.

Shoji, calm… is what she opened her mouth to say. Instead, the screaming she could hear came to stick in her own throat. It filled her lungs, tearing through her body, someone else's screams trapped in her body. Yuki needed to help but the scream in her body pinned her to the spot. Another whistle cut the air, another jet of torn foliage and dirt streamed up into the air. Small rocks pelted her skin leaving welts.

Yuki was grabbed by the shoulders and jerked backwards, still screaming, into the house. It was her father. He pulled her in and nearly threw her onto the bed before latching the back door. Her mother pulled her in close, wrapping her arms around both Yuki and her brother. Shoji wasn't moving, just a small ball of little boy, his naked back exposed beneath their mother's arm. In the shock of being thrown, Yuki had stopped screaming. She wrapped her arms around Shoji to help her mother protect him.

In another minute, her father was there too. He pulled the bedding up around them as if the bits of cloth and cotton could somehow protect against the whistling madness that was tearing the world apart beyond their door. Yuki wasn't screaming now, none of them made any noise at all except Shoji. His face was buried so far under blankets all she could hear from him was low wails. Someone was trembling violently but Yuki couldn't tell if it was herself, her parents or all of them.

She released her brother long enough to pull the shiisaa from her pockets, one in her right hand and the other in her left. She squeezed them hard, and whispered pleas into the knot of fear that was her family. *Please make it go away...please protect us...please make it go away...*

And then it *was* over. All the explosions stopped, but the silence was worse than the barrage of noise. None of them moved. Eventually, Yuki's father got up stiffly. No one spoke. He went to the door and peeked through the crack for a few minutes before opening it. From where she sat, Yuki could see the house across from theirs was gone.

Gone wasn't quite accurate. The remains of the house were there. A shell had hit one half of it. Broken beams jutted out of rubble like bones. The small stove had been blown out of the house and sat on its side where the animal pens had been. There was no sign of the animals.

They looked on in shocked silence until Mother gave a choked noise. Kaneko, Mrs. Miyagi, had been her friend. Yuki's father stepped outside and closed the door. Mother stood up as well. She went to the back door instead of the front and looked out.

Yuki joined her but she couldn't understand what she was seeing. She was familiar with the view out of the back door, but this was wrong. There was too much sky. It was a dirty shade of gray instead of blue. Together they stood, trying to piece together this reality.

The animals she had just fed this morning were still there, but one of the goats lay on its side in a pool of blood that soaked into the sandy soil. Flies already buzzed around her eyes. A shattered branch punctured the fawn colored hide of the mother goat like a giant's spear. In the corner, her baby bleated helplessly, freshly orphaned. Behind the animal pens the jungle was a chaos of broken trees.

"We should butcher the goat," Mama said finally. Yuki nodded, but neither of them moved. They were still stunned, trying to make sense of things. The world was too quiet. The sky was too big. Finally, strange voices broke them out of their daze. It was men shouting in Japanese.

Yuki and her mother went to the front of the house to better listen. They could hear her father's voice speaking in Japanese back instead of the Uchinaaguuchi everyone else on the island spoke. Mother opened the door just enough for her and Yuki to see out. Behind them, Shoji lay quiet, too shocked to complain. All of the stress was too much for him.

It was soldiers talking to her father. Yuki's Japanese wasn't very good, but she understood enough to know the war was coming. The soldiers told her father to take his family and hide. The Americans would rape his daughters and wife, smash the heads of his babies, and chop off his legs. Yuki's father looked ill.

The Japanese soldier handed her father a small, black cylinder. Her father tried to refuse but the soldier said it was a better death. Father took it, his hand trembling. He didn't tuck it away in his kimono but held it out, as if it were something dirty or he wanted to offer it back. The Japanese soldier shook his head at her father as if he were simple and then pushed past him to speak with other men. Her father stood still, staring at the thing the soldier had given him.

"What is it?" Yuki called softly.

Her voice broke him out of his reverie and he looked from the object to his wife and daughter, still standing in the doorway. Yuki had never seen her father cry. He walked toward them both, holding the round object at arm's length. Tears streamed down his cheeks. Yuki's mother stepped back and scolded him.

"What are you doing? Why did the soldier give you a grenade? Don't bring that in this house. Get rid of it. Get rid of it now!"

He stopped coming toward them and looked confused before going back to the remains of the Miyagi house. He set the grenade carefully next to what had been the door, delicately as if it were a thin shelled egg. Once placed, he hurried back. As soon as he was within earshot Mother hissed at him.

"Why did the soldier give you a grenade? Does he want you to kill your family?"

Yuki's father nodded. Her mother and father stood in the doorway staring at each other in silence. Yuki couldn't breathe. The weight of everything had lodged in her chest where it fought to squeeze out her heart and lungs. Through the open door she watched the Japanese soldiers move out of sight down the path. When they were gone, her mother suddenly became animated.

"Soldiers are stupid. Why would you want to kill your family? This is what soldiers are good for: stupid ideas. What did he say about enemies? I don't understand all his words."

Her father opened his mouth to speak but his voice broke. Concerned, Yuki took his hand, and when he looked at her it was as if he came back to himself. He cleared his throat, wiped the tears away with his free hand and stood up straighter.

"Yes, they have no common sense. He was trying to scare me with stories of the Americans, but they don't understand caves. They don't know how to hide underground. That's what we need to do. We must run and hide in the caves to the north. The Americans are coming from the Southwest."

Yuki's mother was all business now.

"Good, then that is our plan. Yuki, dress yourself and your brother. Our goat is dead. Father, clean her as best you can and we will bring the meat and have a feast. Her baby…" Mama's own voice shook a little, but she recovered quickly. "Her baby will have to be cleaned too. There isn't any good leaving it here alone." Her gaze flitted around the small house. Yuki looked around too. Father went into the back.

She had never thought of her family as rich, but suddenly it felt like their house was full of precious things. The delicate bowls from the mainland, the bamboo spoons her father made, the blankets made of patches her mother had sewn together. Her mother bowed to the sefu utaki on a shelf over their stove. The three stones represented earth, sea and heaven. She rolled them up in a cloth before tucking the bundle away. Instinctively, Yuki's hands went to the two shiisaa tucked safely into her pockets. This was a good time to keep guardians from the other world close to this one.

Her mother turned and clapped her hands to spur Yuki to action.

"Now, Yuki!"

Six

Kaori, North Okinawa, Dreaming

Suddenly, she was back with her little brother the last time she had seen him. They were at the grotto shrine and they had heard voices from behind the waterfall. Kaori had wanted to explore inside the cave and see, but her brother had been too scared. She told him to wait outside, but he'd been scared to do that either. Kaori would have left him crying outside, but she knew he would tell on her. "Just for a minute, Hiro," she had told him. "I just want the spirits talking behind the shrine."

She had ducked behind the curtain of water before he had time to protest. She thought she would just take a quick look and return before he could start crying, but she underestimated her brother's fear. As soon as she vanished behind the curtain he started yelling. In the dim rippling light of the cave, she thought she saw a shadow flit along the wall and vanish deeper. *A spirit!* Kaori crept forward, but outside, Hiro was ramping up his shrill cry.

"Hiro! Be quiet or the spirits will get you!"

Her words had the opposite effect she had hoped for and his wailing started to crescendo. At that moment, Kaori hated him. She rejected every second of his existence, hated every fiber of his being. Were it not for this monster coming into her world, her life would have been perfect. Determined, she turned her back and started toward the bend with the intention of just taking a fast look before returning. Outside, Hiro continued to scream.

Furious, Kaori spun around to yell at her little brother, but she slipped on the wet stones and fell. A bolt of pain shot up to her elbow from her wrist. "Hiro! Just go away. No one wants you!" Hiro finally went silent. Kaori had been relieved. She'd rolled onto her knees and carefully regained her footing.

Taking advantage of Hiro's silence, she crept to the back of the cave where she thought she'd seen something. Of course, there was nothing—no spirit. If there had been, it would have been scared away by all the noise. Disappointed, Kaori slipped back through the curtain of water. Hiro was gone.

That had been a year ago. She never saw Hiro again until this dream. They were back at the grotto, and once again they had heard the voices but this time Kaori would not go in. This was her chance to redeem herself and save her family the sorrows she had caused. Hiro stood with his back to the waterfall, the same as that day, and Kaori loved him. The voices drifted from behind the water, but Kaori paid them no mind.

"Hiro!"

She gathered him into her arms, hugging his little baby body that stubbornly held on some toddler plumpness. "I love you so much. I'm so sorry for everything."

"Kaori, can you hear the spirits?"

"Yes, yes. But it doesn't matter. I have you back and I'm sorry. I take it back. I always want you."

"You have to speak with them, Kaori."

His voice wasn't as she remembered. He didn't sound like a small boy with a hint of giggle and whine in his words. He sounded serious. He sounded… adult. Kaori's heart started pattering at the base of her throat.

"I'm not going, Hiro. You need to come home. Mama is waiting for you."

"No, Mama is across the sea. She weeps for us. You watched her go."

Kaori carefully let go of what she had mistaken for her baby brother and stepped back. He was looking at the stones on the ground, not at Kaori. He stood too still for a little boy.

"Where is Hiro?"

"Kaori, speak to the spirits. They call you."

Kaori stepped back further. It looked like her little brother, but there was nothing of a child about him. The temperature in the grotto dropped. Kaori's skin prickled with cold sweat and she shivered.

"Give back my brother, please. I didn't mean what I said."

"I'm right here, Kaori. I'm still with you. Speak to the spirits."

"Give me back my bro—"

What looked like Hiro finally raised his gaze to fix on Kaori. His eyes were liquid black. It was like looking into the night sky. Even the whites had vanished into that galactic pool.

"Speak to the spirits!"

In shock, Kaori stepped back and once again slipped on the rocks to fall backwards. She hit the ground, all the breath knocked out of her and sat back up quickly to face Not-Hiro. But Not-Hiro was no longer there. Neither was the grotto, the waterfall or the whispering spirit voices.

Kaori was back on the beach, frozen and covered in damp sand. Her midsection was cramping like a knife slicing her open from hip bone to hip. The sun rose up behind the tree line and birds were beginning their morning duets. Kaori stood up, gritting her teeth against the pain in her lower belly. As it became day, she would be exposed on the bare expanse of sand. Even in the water she wouldn't be able to hide from anyone watching from the trees.

She had to find some place to hide—someplace neither soldiers nor enormous beasts could go.

Seven

Shigeko, Zamami Island, A Long Walk

Normally it was a short walk to the monument, but today was not normal. It took several hours to go the distance. There were strange smells and sounds on the island. Men shouting, explosions and the smell of heated steel overpowered the green scents Shigeko was used to.

Father made them walk to the side of the wide, stone lined road where the undergrowth made progress slow. The road was a place for people going somewhere to stroll and chat beneath the shady Banyan trees that grew along the edge.

Today it was a passage of fear. Several times Shigeko's father made them leave the road entirely to hide. Tension turned every face into a stranger's mask. The fear affected them all, but poor Chiga fared the worst. Trying to be brave, he kept his tears to himself. He kept his head down for most of it, but Shigeko could hear his sniffles and see the streaks left behind on his baby cheeks.

They were still traveling by late afternoon when they heard engines rattling up ahead. Shigeko's father shuffled them off the road to hide in the brush right before a group of six Japanese soldiers rode through on motorbikes. Their clumsy machines wobbled over the rough road. The soldiers shouted at the villagers that were walking along the edge, yelling at them to hurry up and get to the monument.

An old woman hobbled along the edge of the stone road, the edges of the forest too tangled for her to navigate without a stick to support herself. Two of the soldiers stopped and got off their motorbikes when they saw her.

"Why do you go so slowly, Grandmother?" one asked in his strange tongue. Shigeko couldn't understand every word of their Japanese, but she caught the meaning. The other soldier laughed and kicked at her stick.

"Why bother going at all at this pace? You'll die of old age before you arrive."

Father motioned for them to all crouch deeper into the tree line, hidden from the road by shadows. Mother looked at him and gestured to the old woman but he shook his head.

"I have my family to protect," he whispered.

On the road, through the trees Shigeko could see the other soldiers had stopped and gotten off their bikes as well. The grandmother was surrounded by soldiers, all jeering at her. One tried to grab her stick but she twisted it out of his hands and knocked him in the head, hard. He was surprised enough that he fell back on his bottom. Chiga giggled and was shushed by his mother. Shigeko couldn't blame him. She almost laughed out loud herself. The soldier looked like an angry, uniformed baby sitting in the middle of the road with his legs out straight.

With the other soldiers laughing at him, he scrambled to his feet and shoved the elderly woman so hard she fell back. Shigeko could hear the crack of her frail bones on the stone road. Shigeko's father made a move forward now, but this time it was her mother that held him back.

She shook her head no. "You have a family to protect."

The soldier kicked at the woman that lay on the ground, his foot connecting with her middle. Shigeko wrapped her arms around Chiga to hide the violence from his sight and buried her face into his thick hair. He smelled of little boy sweat and grass. She tried not to hear the sound of the old woman as she cried out. Shigeko counted three cries before the other soldiers pulled him away.

The soldiers exchanged angry words over the old woman before hopping back on their motorcycles to ride on. When the sound of motors had completely faded, Shigeko's family hurried to help the old woman. Other people came out of the forest and Shigeko realized her family wasn't the only one to watch and do nothing. Surprisingly, the old woman seemed unhurt. They helped to her feet and returned her walking stick. She spat angrily in the direction the soldiers had gone.

"This is who will protect us from the war? We should all kill ourselves now. I can't believe I stayed alive for this. A group of bullies." The old woman spat again in the direction of the soldiers. There was sticky blood on the back of her head, darkening red against her white hair. Shigeko was surprised the old woman didn't act more hurt. *Maybe anger dulls her pain.*

They soon came to where the road was paved and walking was faster, even with the old woman slowing them. They made good time until they heard more soldier voices ahead. Without a word, they all scattered back into the woods. Shigeko glanced back fearfully for the old woman and was relieved to see that she had hidden this time as well. A group of soldiers marched past, several dozen on foot. When they were out of sight, the islanders returned to the road.

It was late afternoon by the time the group arrived at the Monument to the Loyal Dead. People ahead of them stood in a long line waiting. At the head were Japanese soldiers surrounded by wooden crates. The long, slow walk was over, but it did nothing to ease Shigeko's nerves. She kept her jaw clenched to keep her complaints and fear locked inside. Her teeth ached from it. She held a smile for Chiga, but she wondered if the smile was worse than just letting him see her fear.

"What are they giving us?" Her little brother was interested in the mystery gifts being distributed.

Shigeko didn't know, but her insides twisted with dread. At the head of the line she saw people receive something from the soldiers and, after a few words, their shoulders would bow beneath the weight of it. Mothers and fathers gathered their children to them. Older people scolded.

"Is it candy?" Chiga asked.

Father stared straight ahead with a stiff posture.

"It is a gift of honor."

His face was frightening, not the sometimes stern but always loving father Shigeko knew. This man had a hard look in his eyes, a cruelty. Shigeko's mother made a soft noise as if to hush him but he refused to be quiet.

"It is true. We can not protect our children from this. Better they know what could be ahead so they face it like soldiers."

"My children are not soldiers." Shigeko had never heard her mother snap like that. "Neither is my husband." Her eyes flashed in anger.

She had stepped in front of Shigeko and Chiga, blocking them from their father's view. He looked angrier than she had ever seen him. His jaw was so tight she could see muscles popping under the skin. Shigeko thought her parents were about to fight. They glared at each other, eye to eye, shoulders squared. Then her father's shoulders slumped. He stepped back.

"You are right." His voice was low, a murmur. Around them, other people in line averted their eyes to be polite. Mother relaxed and put her arms around his shoulders. He pressed his hand over hers, holding it to his cheek as if asking her to check for fever.

"If they did fight, Mother would win." Chiga said in a loud whisper. That broke the tension and everyone laughed, including Shigeko and her parents. The line moved up, and they did as well.

Shigeko looked ahead to the Monument. She had been here many times. It was a place of festivals to honor those that had gone before. The tall stone tablet commanded respect, but also contributed to the sense of community. It was here they gathered to eat, dance and play since as long as she could remember.

Today was not that kind of gathering. Everyone looked despondent. Small children cried and mothers absently nursed their babies while they all shuffled forward. Shigeko was scared. She put her hands into her pockets and felt for her shiisaa. She squeezed them against her palms, willing them to come to life and protect them all. Chiga was fretting so she gave him the boy shiisaa to hold. They both needed some comfort.

"Do you remember the story of how shiisaa came to be our protectors?"

Her mother told them both this story many times. It was a favorite. Shigeko sat Chiga in the grass and they placed both shiisaa between them to listen. Her mother smiled at her thankfully.

"A long time ago a diplomat came to visit the king in Shuri Castle. He'd been told what a fine people the islanders were, the most hospitable of people. He brought the king a gift, the first shiisaa. It was a single little lion dog amulet for protection. Just one, maybe the male. The king immediately knew what a strong talisman this was and he always wore it.

"One day he was visiting a village to examine reports of a great dragon that attacked from the sea. While he was standing on the beach, the very same dragon rose up from the waters before him. A wise yuta woman in the village had a dream of this happening and knew what to do. She had been watching and waiting for the right time. When the dragon rose up before the king, she sent a boy to tell the king what to do.

"'Hold your shiisaa up high so the dragon can see it,' he told him. 'The wise woman says so.'

"The king did as the boy instructed. He pulled his amulet free and held it high so the dragon could see it. Immediately the dragon reared up, afraid of the power in the tiny shiisaa.

"Just then a large, flaming stone fell from the sky and pinned the dragon to the ocean floor. He thrashed to free himself but it was no help. He was trapped and eventually he died. Dirt and trees settled over him. Today he is stuck there still as 'Gana-mui Woods' near Naha Ohashi bridge. Since the king had to return to Shuri Castle with his protective shiisaa amulet, the people of the village built a single large shiisaa for themselves from stone. This was the first shiisaa. It faces out onto the ocean and protects the people still. This is why dragons don't dare attack us from the sea anymore."

Chiga's eyes were shining. This story was his personal favorite.

"And what was the boy's name? You didn't say what his name was!" He raised his voice for the benefit of anyone in ear shot. He was bouncing on his heels with excitement.

Shigeko made him wait, letting his excitement build before finishing the story.

"I believe the boy was named…" She paused and tapped her temple as if trying to jog her memory. "Something that sounded like…" She snapped her fingers trying to remember.

"Chiga! The boy was Chiga! Like my name!"

Chiga yelled out loud. Even the soldiers at the head of the line glanced up at them.

"Yes, the hero that saved them all was named Chiga."

Her own Chiga was happy again. He occupied himself with her shiisaa, marching them around in the grass, building a miniature shrine for them with small sticks and stones. Her parents had moved a few feet up in line but she stayed behind while Chiga was happily occupied. She wondered if dragons were returning to the island again. Dragons with steel hearts of fire and bellies full of men. She hoped the shiisaa would continue to protect them.

A man walked by with his wife and three daughters, and Shigeko finally got to see what they were passing out at the end of the line. It was a small, iron cylinder that looked like a black fruit. At the top was a thin metal fork attached to a cord. Shigeko recognized it from pamphlets they had read in school. She looked up at her mother in shock. She was watching the family as well and their eyes met.

The three little girls were pestering their father to let them touch the explosive as if it was something special. Their father held it high, out of their reach.

"What is it? What is it?" the youngest yelled, hopping up in an attempt to touch it. Her father pushed her down with one hand and gave her a warning rap on her head to calm down.

"It is a gift of honor," he said.

Shigeko sat down behind Chiga and gathered him in her arms. Holding him as he held her shiisaa, she prayed.

Please, please keep the dragons away. Please protect us again.

Eight

Yuki, South Okinawa, Growing Up

❧

Yuki listened to the pitiful bleating of the little goat kid in the back of the house. It gave a squeal and then was silent. She choked back her tears and set to gathering things for Shoji and herself. She didn't know how long they would be gone so she must be wise. A whispering voice at the back of her mind said they might never return.

Within an hour, they were heading to the caves. The family walked single file down the road. Yuki's father led the way with all the goat he could carry wrapped in a sheet on his back. He hadn't had time to drain the animals properly so the blood seeped through. Knowing they were in a situation where their mother would allow their bedding to be ruined was the most frightening thing of all.

Mama followed, a few woven bags slung around her shoulders and a whining Shoji on her back. Normally he would have been made to walk, but they needed to move faster than little boy legs allowed. Mama also carried her pan in the bags. Yuki could hear it banging like a muffled gong.

Following last, Yuki carried the bundles of clothes they would need. Since the spring nights were still cool, Mama instructed her to pack the cotton kimono as well as the light bashofu ones. She was pretty sure Mama had woven their family's kimono from the basho leaves, but it was a long process that the women of the village worked together on.

While the weaving was done as individuals, turning the thick, green banana leaves into the light, summery cloth took many people and a few years. When she was Shoji's age, Yuki thought bashofu was made from the wings of dragonflies because of the name. The bashofu did feel light and airy, like wings, compared to the heavier, cotton bundles.

Other people joined them on the march to the caves. Many of them Yuki knew well. Others seemed familiar but only in passing. A few were complete strangers. It was unusual to see a face she had never met. They all carried makeshift bundles. In a stream, they were all heading the same direction.

Even though she was nearly 14, Yuki didn't recall ever being so far away from her home. When they stopped for a meal break, her father said they would go to a place he knew in the far north, as far away from the Americans as possible. There was a large cave that would have plenty of room for them all. They could stay there, safe, while the soldiers were on the island.

"Why are they here?" Yuki asked. "What do they want?"

Her father was silent, making a big deal out of chewing his sweet potato. Finally, he swallowed.

"I'm not sure, Yuki. I think they want to fight the Japanese."

"Let them fight then," snapped Mama. "That has nothing to do with us but it's our goat killed. Who will pay for the goat? The Japanese? The Americans? They shouldn't bring us into their problems."

Around them, there were murmurs of agreement. The place they had stopped was a shady clearing with some rocks and stumps to sit on. Quite a few of their fellow travelers took advantage of this with them. One of the women passed around a small, paper bag of kokuto. The brown sugar rocks were a treat. Shoji was asleep but the woman told Yuki to take two, one for herself and one for her brother. Yuki did as she was told, popping one in her mouth and the other between her thumb and forefinger so she wouldn't get sticky in the heat.

The sugar was rich and sweet. There was no sugar like it in the world, she had heard people say. Yuki could believe it. There was a hint of sea salt in the aftertaste that stayed on her tongue. After her candy was dissolved the woman rolled the paper bag up and gave it to Mama for later. She winked at Yuki and smiled.

"You should carry the one you are holding in your mouth so the ants don't smell it and carry you away. Your mother will make sure your brother gets his share when he wakes up." The woman's face was kind, but despite her smile she looked sad. Her hair was loose, as if she had hurried too fast to put it up before they left, but a large, jade circle hung from a black cord around her neck as if she were heading somewhere special. Yuki ate the second sugar lump and thanked her. Then the woman rejoined the line of people moving along the path.

Yuki's father wanted to hurry and move on, but Mama was tired. She had carried Shoji most of the way along with her pan, potatoes and some extra clothes. Yuki's father carried the goat meat, but in the heat it wasn't going to last much longer without cooking it. Her parents discussed it in low voices. Her father wanted to leave it there and get to the caves. Her mother wanted him to cook it and take it with them. They went back and forth in tense voices, unable to come to an agreement until her father put his arms around Mama and held her close.

"The soldiers are coming. We can replace the goats. We can't replace…"

He stopped speaking, but they both glanced where Yuki sat, holding Shoji, still groggy from sleep. The sentence hung in the air unfinished, but her father set the bloody bundle of goat down at the foot of a tree to leave it behind.

Yuki remembered all the times she had sat outside daydreaming in the goat pen, listening to the sound of chewing and soothing bleats. It wasn't like losing Shoji or Mama, but it was a loss of life just the same. All that was left of the goat with her soft brown eyes was a bundle of bloody meat swarming with flies. The day dimmed as a cloud crossed before the sun, and it felt like prophesy. Yuki thought of herself wrapped up in old bedding like that, bleeding, and then she was crying.

Mama took action.

"Now stop. You are too old for weeping."

Frightened by his sister's tears and over tired, Shoji started crying too.

Along the path, travelers turned their eyes away. Yuki wanted to compose herself, but the more she tried to stop the sobs, the more they took over. She started gasping, unable to breathe. Next to her, Shoji was in full wail, clinging to Mama's kimono and pulling on her.

Mama pulled out the paper bag of candy and caught Shoji's attention. His bawling subsided to sniffles as Mama made a big show out of opening the bag and showing him what was inside. Within minutes he was occupied with seeing how many lumps Mama would let him eat.

Meanwhile, her father came to Yuki, knelt down and put his arms around her. He hadn't held her like that in years. She sobbed into his arm as if she were a baby like her brother, inconsolable. She wrapped her arms around him. There was something strange in the kinchaku bag at his side. As she sobbed she felt it without thinking, trying to figure out what it was. It was like a narrow can but the texture was strange. The shell had an etched pattern, like lines in a grid.

Shocked out of her sobs, she jerked her hand away and sat back. It was the grenade the Japanese soldier had given her father. She thought he had left it outside of the Miyagi's house—what was left of the house. Instead, he had it on him, hidden. His eyes met hers. She had never seen her father look so sad.

"Just in case, Yuki. It's for just in case. But let's not mention it to anyone else, okay?"

Yuki just nodded. Her insides were cold and calm now. A numbness drifted over her as if all of this wasn't real. She was just a heroine in a story. Soon, Mama would shake her awake and scold her for sleeping in too long. Yuki would go out and give the goats the sweet smelling sea grass. The trees around their home would once again block out the sky and filter the ocean breeze. She would look through the crack in the front door and see the corner of her neighbor's house. A dream—that's all this could be. For her father to have a grenade in his bag...Yuki couldn't believe that was real.

She wiped her face dry with her sleeve, stood up and slung her bundles back across her shoulder. Shoji was licking the inside of the paper bag, leaving no pieces of kokuto for her. That certainly felt real. She felt in her pockets for her shiisaa. Her baaban made them for her when she was as old as Shoji was now. She sent out a plea for her grandmother to be with them, even if it were only a bad dream.

"Keep us safe. Watch over us," Yuki whispered. "Please keep us safe."

Neither of her parents spoke as they hefted their burdens and rejoined the foot traffic on the path heading to the north, farther away than she had ever been, but it didn't feel far enough. Behind them, the soldiers might be setting their oversize boots on the island. Danger behind, but close at hand, the conspicuous lump in the bag at her father's side meant there was no place far enough.

Yuki put herself between her parents now, ahead of her mother and Shoji and behind her father. Her insides had chilled. Like winter sand, she felt dense and heavy. Yuki imagined herself as a body bag of soil, shielding her mother and Shoji from the invisible threat behind what bounced carelessly against her father's hip.

As they walked, Yuki felt the familiar recede from her. If she left the small road they walked, she would be lost. She had no sense of direction or time. She wasn't scared, or sad, or even exhausted. Yuki just concentrated on staying on her feet, between her parents, and hoping she would soon wake up.

When the light was slanting through the trees toward sunset, they reached the cave. There were already many people there. Most of them were unfamiliar to her. Mama and Shoji found a clear spot and dropped to the ground, happy to rest. Yuki stood awkwardly, not knowing what to do among all the strangers. Her father walked to the entrance of the cave, almost hidden by the hanging branches of a banyan tree.

He spoke at length with some of the men that sat there. The conversation looked grim. None of them laughed or smiled. Her father absently touched the grenade bulge at his side several times while they spoke, as if to reassure himself it was still there. Finally, he returned.

Yuki watched how he walked back to them. He was hunched over as if the soil was pulling him down to meet it. He moved slowly, paused halfway and looked back at the cave before turning slowly to look around at the group gathered with a lost expression on his face. When he saw Yuki watching him, he smiled but his eyes remained dark. He walked to his family and shrugged as if to de-emphasize the impact of his words.

"So, we walked too slow. They say there is already no room inside the cave."

His eyes were on Shoji who was busy trying to build a corral for a beetle with tiny sticks and stones. He didn't look to his wife or daughter. Mama didn't say anything for a few minutes. Her skin was translucent and ashen. She looked fragile. Finally, she spoke.

"Then we can sleep out here, under the stars for tonight. Tomorrow we will walk on and find another place. If this island is wealthy in anything, it is caves. Too bad those don't export well. We would be a wealthy people."

This seemed to break her father free from his despair. He chuckled and smiled at her with returning warmth and sat on the ground next to her. Motioning to them all, he gathered Shoji and Yuki into his arms. They sat huddled together like that for a few minutes. Her father and mother planted kisses on her head. Shoji protested that his beetle was trying to escape.

Yuki wanted to reach around to pat the grenade in her father's bag. The cylinder of harm obsessed her. It looked like some strange fruit. She imagined what it would taste like—fire and ash? Her tongue would turn to charcoal in her mouth behind blackened teeth.

She thought again of the bundle of goat they had left behind. She saw it clearly; the cloth sticky with blood, the swarming flies. She could still smell the meat beginning to turn foul in the heat. She remembered the nanny goat and how she would nuzzle her hand, butting to get scratches. The soft, brown eyes... and then the goat dying with the shard of tree piercing her side.

The forest was spinning. Caught in the embrace, Yuki struggled to stay upright on her knees. She was wedged between her parents, leaning on them as her vision started to gray. The edges went first. The murmurings of the people around them faded as her fingertips and tongue went numb. Her world was narrowing once again into one of the crippling headaches that had been plaguing her for the last few months. She had a glimpse of her mother looking at her, worried.

"My head again…" That's all Yuki could get out before the iron rod inserted itself once again behind her left eye, skewering her brain. Then she was sliding free of them to curl on the ground, the dimming evening a sudden shrieking symphony of light and noise. The voices of those gathered amplified into a shouting throng that bounced off the inside of her skull, creating waves of nausea. Then she vomited onto the ground, in front of the crowd of strangers, before she felt her mother pulling her free of the sick and wrapping her in a makeshift bed.

Yuki curled into a ball of pain and slid her hand into her pockets, groping for the two shiisaa she knew waited there. She listened for their song, the rhythmic *aum* that could wrap around the pain in her head and carry it away. The song came in with her waves of nausea, flowing in until she thought it would bury her and then ebbing back out. Each time, the *aum* grew stronger until it overtook the pain. With each ebb, it drew the ache away to somewhere else.

Her world narrowed to this ocean of suffering. Outside of herself she was aware that her family worried. She heard Shoji ask if she was going to die. She wanted to comfort him but she was trapped in herself, blind and mute. This was the fourth time she had experienced the headaches that came on so fast and final. This was the second in two days. She wondered along with Shoji… was she going to die?

You can see in the dark…

The voice soothed through her mind, cooling and sweet like starlight. It smoothed the inside of her aching skull, dampening the hurt. It was the freshening breath of a storm, the cleansing before chaos.

Yuki knew this voice. She heard it plenty when she was young and imagined her shiisaa could speak. She had been barely older than Shoji.

You are remembering to hear…

The other shiisaa, the male. His voice was deeper and golden like brass. It was warm, morning after a cold night, uncoiling her. The pain subsided as they sang. Relaxing, exhausted, Yuki slipped into sleep and dreamt of an endless night full of stars. Yuki slipped into waves of peace.

Nine

Kaori, North Okinawa: The Grotto

Hoping any soldiers would still be asleep, Kaori made a beeline for the relative safety of the trees, but as soon as she reached the shade of the first branches she stopped. She had known the island forests all her life and never felt fear of them—until now. Where had the ferocious shiisaa from last night been hidden all her life? Had it come with the soldiers? Kaori wondered if it was a spirit that was called by what she had done to Hiro.

Nerves strung tight, she crept forward making no sound. She gave a wide berth to hanging branches, flinching when they brushed her skin. Her ears pricked on high alert, hypersensitive, every rustle and twig pop a direct assault on her nerves.

Just days ago the only terrible thing on the island was herself. She had thought of herself as a monster. Now that she had seen real monsters, she knew she wasn't the monster she had thought she was.

Not nearly far enough away, Kaori heard the voices of men. The soldiers were waking up. She was hungry, tired, half naked and chafed from sand. She recognized this beach and knew she could find her home. There was food there. She had spare clothes. She might unroll her little bed and sleep, but it was far from hidden. Home wouldn't be safe. Was anywhere safe?

47

Kaori headed to the only other place she could think of to go—the grotto where she had lost Hiro. Perhaps she could apologize to the spirits. She thought of her mother and father… of the baby that was their latest hope for joy. She hoped they had made it somewhere safe.

On a normal day she could go from one end of the island to the other in about an hour. It took her a full hour just to make her way across the short distance to the grotto. Behind every tree was a potential danger. It felt like soldiers were everywhere. While she didn't see any of them, their voices drifted in the air at a distance. The scent of them clung to the island's breath, tainting it with the whir and grind of machine and the rat-ta-tat of gunfire. Several times she panicked and hid in the underbrush.

Finally she reached the base of the cliffs. Cut by ancient hands straight through solid stone beyond an old grove of fruit trees, the path to the grotto was not easily seen. Kaori didn't think the soldiers would find it, so she would at least be safe from them. That path was narrow, slippery and steep. Perhaps a giant shiisaa couldn't navigate such a climb. That left only angry spirits for her to contend with. At this point, they seemed the safest danger.

The final few steps proved to be the biggest challenge. As she slipped into the grove, she became acutely aware of how a ring of stone surrounded the small grove. Every outcropping seemed to wear the shiisaa's grin. The trees were planted evenly spaced here. They stood in two rows in a narrow pocket so the only way to the grotto was to walk through the middle of them. It was orderly—intentional. It occurred to her that this may have once been an utaki, a place of worship. If so, she deserved to be condemned.

How many times had she played here with her brother? Some of the trees grew mango and they would toss the rotting fruit at each other, slipping and rolling in the grass. When they were too sticky they would make their way to the falls in the grotto and wash themselves. Springing from a source deep in the earth, the water was always cool and fresh. It sprang out of a crevice higher up in the cliffs and rained down in a shower of froth and glittering rainbow into the pool. Her mother had said water from the pool flowed to the sea and was the source of all the waters of Earth. Kaori needed those waters now to wash away her fear and exhaustion.

Tired, skin rubbed raw from sand and scratched from her repeated dives into the underbrush, the cool privacy of the waterfall was a gift. If she was lucky, there would be star fruit. She could wash in the healing waters, eat and then rest on the cool stone. She could figure out what to do. She just had to get through the grove.

It felt as if the stones surrounding the grove were tensing, waiting for her. They were suddenly sentient—too still. Protected from the elements, there was never much air movement in this narrow crevice, but now that stillness felt oppressive. The trees held their breath, waiting for her to pass. Kaori took a deep breath of her own. Safety, rest and refreshment waited just through the grove. She had done this race dozens of times with Hiro. Before she could change her mind, Kaori forced herself to sprint.

Tapping into the last of her reserves, she dug her bare feet deep into the soft turf. Gravity felt like her enemy. It clung to her, invisible, and she felt like the seconds passed in slow motion. As she passed Kaori imagined she could see the stones transforming into colossal stone haunches ready to spring. Reaching the other end, Kaori turned, gasping for breath to see nothing but a quiet grove, quiet stones. The slicing cramps in her abdomen returned, doubling her over. As soon as the pain had passed, Kaori started up the narrow, stone cut path to the grotto.

She hadn't returned since Hiro had vanished. Everyone searched but no trace of him was found. She never mentioned to anyone how she had given him to the spirits. She was too ashamed. Not a word of blame was directed at Kaori, not that she heard. Not even from her own parents, but Kaori felt it. She knew she was to blame. It was decided that Hiro somehow slipped out of the narrow cuts in the rock and fell into the ocean below.

She had returned and the grotto was as peaceful as ever. Once, it had been her favorite place on the island. Tense, she crept forward and slipped into the water. Her skin was instantly relieved as the sandy grime washed off her raw skin. Urine, the soldier's blood and fear lifted from her to find release in the wide ocean, traveling far from her. Kaori's muscles unwound. She submerged and let the water circulate through her hair.

Once she had scrubbed the filth away, she searched for fruit and was rewarded. Prying the fruit open with her hands she gorged on the sun-warmed sweetness. Once satiated, she took another dip to wash away the juice, and then Kaori was ready to sleep. She found a hollow of dry stone and curled up in it. She felt safe here. The only time this place had given her cause to fear was her own fault. Kaori relaxed, clean and fed, and drifted to sleep in the sun.

The cooling air finally woke her. The sky had waned from azure to washed twilight. Above the grotto rim streaks of gold stretched as if reaching for the curtain of night to draw it closed. She yawned. The soldiers could not stay on her island forever. They had their own homes and families. She could wait here until they left. Her family would return. She could survive this.

Some red blossoms, Hibiscus, were scattered on the rock around her. Some had drifted onto her as she slept. She stood up and shook them off. They clung to her, hanging around her neck in a chain. It was a lei, a string of flower blossoms made into a necklace. She had made many of them for special occasions, or just for play. She hadn't worn this when she entered the grotto shrine. Someone else had put it there.

The waterfall was a shimmering veil in the setting sun. Kaori had never explored past the first natural room. She realized that anything could be further back in the cave. More hibiscus blossoms caught her eye. They were floating in the pool and scattered along the shore. A wreath of blossoms hung over the cascading fall from a jutting stone. Strings of flowers were draped in festoons overhead. With horror, Kaori realized the entire grotto was decorated as if in celebration. It was beautiful, but it meant she wasn't alone.

From beyond the fall, Kaori heard soft voices murmuring. *The spirits—the spirits she had heard that day. The spirits that took Hiro.* She pulled the lei from her neck and tossed it into the pool. "I don't want to offend you. Forgive me."

The murmuring intensified with excitement. Kaori backed along the shore slowly, eyes on the shimmering curtain, and edged toward the rough, stone path that led out. One voice separated from the rest, higher pitched. A voice she recognized—"Kaori, don't go." It was Hiro.

"Hiro! Kaori started toward the fall, fear forgotten. It was he that had strung the flowers, of course. They had done it together many times. "I'm so sorry! Hiro. I'm here. I'm taking you home…"

She was wading into the pool when a low growl echoed out from the cave. It rode the mist in shade and blunted the last fragments of light still playing in the water. She recognized the sound. It was the shiisaa. Kaori stopped moving. The growl came again and something moved inside the cave. Kaori started walking backwards, out of the water, angling again toward the path out. A shadow approached the curtain of water as Kaori found purchase on the stone. A lion dog face, bulbous eyes, flat nostrils and a curly mane emerged from the curtain of water, looking for her. She fled.

Ten

Shigeko, Zamami Island: A Guardian for Chiga

Going home didn't take as long. Once her family had stepped forward to get their gift, they simply walked away. None of them spoke. They didn't try to hide in the underbrush. When holding a grenade, it didn't seem worth hiding anymore. They were holding their own death in their hands. What more could they suffer?

Once at home, Mother put the grenade up on a high shelf, carefully wedged in with rags so it wouldn't roll off. She lectured both children about the importance of not touching it. She told them, if anything, it was a keepsake of war they would never have to use. They may even pass it down to their own families.

"It's not a privilege to hold your own death," she told them. "It's a burden." She looked at their father when she said this. There was a warning in her eyes, a coldness Shigeko had never seen. Suddenly she understood the extent a mother will go to protect her children. Her mother loved him. They were happy together. She would miss him if they were separated. In spite of this love, her children would always come first between them.

Afterwards, Mother packed a small bag of things for each of them. It wasn't much. A change of clothes, some dry oyster crackers in bags, a few apple mangos from their yard. The grenade stayed on the shelf, only to be taken down in case of dire circumstances. By then it was dark. Without speaking, they pulled out the beds and lay down, but Shigeko doubted if any of them slept. Still, somehow she woke up just before dawn.

She lay there in the quiet, trying to make sense of everything. She wondered if this would all just be a story she told her grandchildren someday. Perhaps she would take the grenade down from the shelf to remind them how precious life is. She wondered if anything would change or would it be another long day filled with tension. She got her answer just after the sun rose. Things were definitely different.

Father didn't go to dig the shelters that day. Instead, he made breakfast.

Mother didn't get out of bed until the sun was well up. Used to being rolled out of bed far too early, Shigeko snuggled in the covers to take advantage of the lazy morning but it lasted too long. Her stomach began grumbling. Finally she peeked out of the bedding to see her father sitting cross legged in front of the stove stirring a pot of boiling water, but she couldn't smell food cooking.

Shigeko finally got up. When she looked over her father's shoulder into the pot she saw it was boiled nearly dry. A few small potatoes lay unwashed on the floor in front of him but he was just staring into space, stirring the empty pot. Gently, Shigeko took the stir stick from him. The water bucket was empty so she went outside to refill it. When she came back in, she found her father had laid back down in the bed, on top of the cover with his arm around his wife. Mother lay still with her eyes closed. Her father's were open, staring at nothing. Fighting dread, Shigeko added water to the pot and started breakfast.

Chiga woke up at the smell of food. The siblings ate in silence, trying not to look at their sleeping parents. Shigeko did a few chores while Chiga played quietly in the garden. She hoped her parents were probably using the time alone to talk about what might happen but when she came in, neither had moved. Her father had closed his eyes at least. She wondered what she would do if they were orphaned. Would she be Chiga's mother?

Chiga was still tired from the day before, so in the heat of the afternoon she lay back down with him. There didn't seem much point in being up without their parents. Chiga fell asleep with his head on Shigeko's arm. His hair was sweaty, stuck to his damp forehead. Sometimes he was the most troublesome thing in her life but in this moment he was perfect. It wasn't right that this war would come to him. It made no sense that a perfect little boy like Chiga would know what a grenade looked like—would nap quietly with one just a few feet over their heads. Shigeko craned her neck to look up at it.

It looked like a canister that might hold something special, like spices. The surface was textured with tiny rectangles. They looked like obsidian jewels raised on the black metal surface. The silk bit of cord hanging from the pull fork would make a pretty piece of jewelry braid.

Abruptly, alarms blasted across the island. Chiga sat straight up, his eyes bugging out of his head. His little chest heaved as he fought to catch panicked breaths. That got both parents moving. Mother rolled to her feet so swiftly Shigeko couldn't quite see how she did it. Like a warrior, in one fluid motion she stood and pulled Chiga to his feet.

Shigeko's father was sitting up too, but with his hands over his face as if he were crying. Shigeko looked at her mother but got no answer. She was fidgeting with Chiga's clothes, tying a strip of cloth to him so he wouldn't become separated from her. She glanced at her husband and looked away again. Her face communicated worry and impatience. They had to go.

"Father, we have to go to the shelters!" Chiga was excited now that he was awake. He had played games where he pretended to be a soldier. Now he was going to get his chance. "We're finally going to war!"

Father snapped his head up at that. He almost looked angry. The harsh look tamped down Chiga's enthusiasm only slightly. Father stood up and went to the shelf where the grenade stood, carefully wedged in with rags so it wouldn't roll off, and picked it up. He wrapped it carefully and tucked it carefully in his shirt front.

"We are supposed to go to the school shelter."

None of them moved until Shigeko's father gathered them to him. He wrapped his arms around his family. They stood in the doorway like that for a full minute, embracing. Shigeko wanted to keep this moment forever. Then she felt the hard cylinder in her father's shirt and it brought her back to reality. This was no ordinary embrace. Her father was thinking it might be a last embrace.

"We have to go to the shelter."

Her mother's voice was small, frightened and reluctant. Father released them without a word and pushed them out the door. Shigeko longed for the embrace, but she was also relieved to have a space between her and the grenade at least.

And then, silence. The sirens stopped.

The sudden quiet was more shocking than the screaming sirens. Her family stood in front of their house, confused. Chiga whined.

"We missed the war already?"

Normally this would have been a comical moment, but no one even answered him. Just then, a soldier rode by on a bicycle.

"False alarm. Go home! False alarm!"

He rode through the street, his voice trailing off in the distance as he pedaled away. The common area outside their house was full of their neighbors meandering around, looking tense and confused.

"Go back! Go back home. False alarm!"

A few people took up the call but most stayed outside, gathering into small groups. They kept their voices low as they shared what little info any of them had. Shigeko's mother shooed her children back inside. Chiga was irritable and he stomped around the small house several times before throwing himself on the beds that were still spread out. Shigeko pulled out her shiisaa pair.

"Chiga, will you take care of the boy shiisaa for me?"

Immediately Chiga sat up. All signs of fussiness evaporated from him. He was all smiles.

"Yes! I will take good care of him, Shigeko. You will see. I'll protect him."

She placed the male shiisaa onto Chiga's palm, kissed the little clay shiisaa and then closed Chiga's fingers over it. She kissed his grimy, little boy fingers as well.

"There," she said. "You can be his caretaker for a while and our shiisaa can meet up and go on adventures together."

Shigeko supposed she should just give Chiga the shiisaa, both of them, but they were still too precious to her. Her babaan promised that the shiisaa would always protect her and bring her luck. This was true. There had been so many times in Shigeko's life that the shiisaa gave her a whispered warning not to go down a path or set foot in a patch of grass. Every time she had listened, and each time she was saved from some catastrophe.

Now, she hoped they could protect her and her little brother too.

Eleven

Yuki, South Okinawa: The Landing

The peace didn't last long.

The sound of gunfire from a distance woke her up. Yuki had never heard a gun before, but she knew instinctively what it was. She lay there for a few seconds, relieved to find the pain in her head had gone away. Then the gunfire came again, sharp cracks of sound strung like beads on razor wire. The cicadas went silent. She couldn't judge how close or far. People were stirring around them. A baby cried somewhere. Yuki sat up.

Her mother was already bundling the few things they had left with them. Yuki's stomach rumbled with hunger, but there was no time for that. She rolled to her feet, feeling light and insubstantial but not weak. The absence of pain made her feel strong.

The cracks came again from a distance. Machine guns, but it was hard to tell from what direction or how far away. Yuki thought maybe south, from the direction they had just come. The entire camp was stirring now, all the people that slept under the stars scrambling to pack up their things as well. Yuki helped her mother. Her father was already gone.

"He is asking once again if there is room enough for us," said Mama. "He wastes time. If there was room, these people would be in there as well."

Yuki wanted to ask about the grenade. Did her mother know about it? Did she think it was okay?

A bundle of sleepy Shoji was thrust into her arms. He was hot and cranky. He pushed at her face, complaining. The gunfire came again, far away. Shoji stopped fussing instantly and stared into her face with big eyes.

"What was that?"

Yuki patted his back to soothe him.

"Firecrackers. There is a celebration going on. We are traveling to see it."

She was worried Mama would scold her for the lie, but instead she looked at Yuki with a smile, thin and weak. There were shadows under her eyes. As she knotted a cloth, Yuki could see her hands were shaking.

"Yes, a fun celebration! We just need your father to stop obsessing over the damn cave!"

Her voice cracked as she jerked the ends of the cloth viciously. She threw the bundle onto the ground in frustration and turned away from her children. Her shoulders shook as she tried to compose herself. Yuki wanted to comfort her, but her arms were full of Shoji.

"Is Mama okay?" he asked.

Yuki nodded at him. "Yes, she's excited to go to the celebration but we need Father to come back." Yuki tried to look calm but her stomach felt like it was becoming unlaced. Any moment she felt it might fall out onto the ground. She scanned the area around them, looking for her father.

The area was dark. No one had built a fire. There were shadows everywhere in small groups, scurrying to move on. Yuki didn't know how many caves there were on the island, but by now they must all be filled. She hadn't known there were this many people on the whole island. Mother got a hold of her emotions, finished packing and stood waiting.

"Where is your father?"

Her voice had a shrill edge to it. Yuki suspected the laces holding her mother's stomach together were also becoming unraveled. Perhaps when her father returned there would be nothing left of either of them, just Shoji left alone with the remains of his family around him..

The machine gun fire broke out again, but not as distant. Yuki thought she could hear screams mixed in with the staccato pops. Without meaning to, her grip on Shoji tightened to the point he gave a squeal of pain. Yuki let him slide down to stand on his own feet but she refused to let go of his hand. Her heart was thudding in her chest, knocking the air out of her. The soldiers were coming.

"Where is your father?"

Mama said this too loud and her voice shook. Even Shoji picked up on the raw panic threaded through her voice. As if in answer, more gunfire. This time Yuki was sure she heard cries mixed in. The gunfire stopped, but one voice continued. It was a wail, not of pain but of loss. A woman's voice rose up above the trees, caught up in the wind and flew among them in the light of the nearly full moon. All who heard it were infected. No one moved as they listened, horrified by the wail. Then more gunfire and the voice was cut short.

"He will find us. We must go now. Yuki, carry bags and I will take Shoji. We need to go fast."

Mama looked around again, desperate to see her husband. Yuki scanned as well. Surely her father was coming. Any second he would be hurrying out of the shadows toward them. Then Mama was scooping Shoji into her arms, grabbing Yuki by her shoulder and spurring them forward.

As if everyone had the same thought, the people camping nearby started scattering. There was no tired march along the road now. In the dark, people were tripping over abandoned goods. Just a few feet away to her left, Yuki saw a woman trip so badly she dropped her baby. A running man tripped over the baby and stumbled to his knees.

Yuki ran to them without thinking and scooped the screaming infant up to safety. The woman snatched the baby from Yuki and stumbled away. More gunfire, even closer, and Yuki jumped and turned to run, but where? In the jumble of fleeing bodies, Mama and Shoji were gone. She panicked.

"Mama! Shoji!"

Yuki couldn't pick out their voices in the mix of cries and yells. People ran into her in the dark, but the area had cleared out. In the forests all around her she could hear bodies crashing through the underbrush.

There were dangerous smells in the air. Iron tainted smoke, burning poisons—the smell of strangers.   Again, the sharp reports of gunfire interspersed with screams. Above the trees there was smoke. The soldiers were here.

Twelve

Kaori, North Okinawa: Homecoming

Kaori's feet barely touched the ground as she sped through the narrow stone cut in panic. Kaori ran blind, no thought to where she was going. Into the forests, across the wind flattened expanses of beach, she fled. Soldiers, her brother, her parents… all were forgotten in the immediate need to escape the terror that had claimed the one safe place left to her.

It was only when she heard a woman's keening in the distance, crying from intense loss, that she stopped. More gunfire and the woman's cries were cut short. Kaori remembered the other dangers all around her. In her mindless flight she was running home out of habit. She was already near the small creek that ran behind their house. She had played in it many times, digging small crabs out of the mud. Home was no longer a safe place to go, and yet Kaori crept closer.

She could smell smoke and in the darkening sky she could see flames flickering in the distance. Her house was closer. They weren't there yet. She could slip in, snatch food, a change of clothes, and be gone. Her long shirt acted as a short dress but trousers would be better. Perhaps she could find a boat and follow her parents. She could still escape these soldiers.

But she had heard Hiro's voice in the grotto, and to leave would be deserting him to the spirits that held him. It was the shiisaa, she now knew. That's what lived in the cave. That's what she had given her brother to. Maybe it was even her evil deed that had called the soldiers to their island. Maybe it was her selfishness that brought the shiisaa to punish her.

War was a tale traders brought home, not a thing her people had known first hand. Something had upset the balance and that something was her. What kind of person would give a small boy to the spirits? What kind of sister would abandon her baby brother to a beast?

Kaori remembered how the shiisaa had held his giant paws out to her. She had taken it as a threat but in reflection it didn't seem aggressive. It was more like an embrace. Perhaps the shiisaa wished she had offered herself instead. Maybe he needed a helper, or someone to take care of the grove. Maybe the shiisaa would take a trade. Perhaps she could make things right after all.

"I can save him. I can undo this. I can offer myself in trade. I can fix this. I'll bring a gift as an apology. I can save Hiro."

She could see her house now, dark and lonely in the sandy little clearing where she had always lived. Her home looked strange sitting so quiet and dark. It was always lit up at this time as they ate together. Even after Hiro was gone they had been a family. Kaori's eyes blurred.

The soldiers had not gotten there yet but the pigs had smelled her. They were already grunting and rooting in anticipation that she was bringing scraps. They would starve to death locked up. She could fix this too.

Kaori crept forward in the dark. She went to the pigs first and opened the pen. Tame and hungry, they didn't run away but followed her, squealing for food. She would get them some. Quietly, she slipped into the house and closed the door on the squealing pigs.

Inside was as she had last seen it. Rice was spilled across the floor in the rush. The basket of vegetables had tipped over. Kaori gathered some wilted greens and melons and threw them out the door to hush the pigs, but they only squealed louder now that they knew there was food.

"Be quiet!" Kaori gave a low whistle to distract, but.the pigs were inconsolable. She drug the basket to the door, opened it and started rolling sweet potatoes out at them. The pigs only squealed louder in their excitement at the abundance of food.

A shout sounded from nearby, and then answering yells. The soldiers were in the clearing! Kaori had to get back into the woods. She could hide in the grotto. The enemy of her enemy, the shiisaa may even protect her. Shiisaa were protectors, after all. She had never heard of a demon shiisaa.

She tried to pull the door open but the turned over basket was in the way. The pigs were pushing in the doorway to get at the spilled bounty. Kaori tripped as she tried to push past the cluster of excited pigs. On the ground she threw her arms over her head to protect her face from the hungry swine. She crawled forward like that, pushing her way free of the pigs that were now entering the house. Their hooves bit into her back as they trampled her.

The sound of a gunshot deafened her. One of the pigs screamed and the rest scattered. Stunned, Kaori lay still as the panicked animals fled. She looked up to see one of the piglets on its side, a gash in the soft pink skin bubbling blood as it gasped and kicked feebly. Just a few feet beyond, stood a soldier with a gun barrel trained on her. Kaori buried her face in her hands. She was going to die.

The soldier yelled in his flat dialect and suddenly there were soldiers everywhere. One of them roughly grabbed her up by her arm. Her long shirt rode up exposing her and they all laughed. She couldn't understand their words but the meaning was clear. The one that held her jerked her shirt hard until it tore part way. The one with the gun poked her bare bottom with it. Kaori shrieked at them and kicked as she was drug into the house. The rest of her shirt tore free and Kaori tumbled naked back into her own house.

The small, one room hut was suddenly filled with tall men in uniforms. They surrounded her, grinning with flushed faces and licking their flat lips. Kaori scooted to the back of the hut and wrapped her arms around herself, hunched over and trying to hide her exposed body. The cramps in her belly returned like a hot blade slicing into her.

The soldier with the gun handed it to one of his companions and stepped forward, unbuckling his pants. Kaori snarled at him but he just smiled at her and said something that made them all laugh. In her fear, Kaori felt liquid running down her legs. That was too much humiliation. She had wet herself like a baby before these hateful men.

The soldier coming towards her had stopped. He looked disgusted. All the soldiers started yelling, laughing and pointing at her. One of them threw a torn part of her shirt at her. She snatched up the shirt to wipe away the urine and saw she had not peed herself at all. She was bleeding. She had just become a woman. It was a special moment, but to have it happen now in front of these savage men was the worst possible fate Kaori could imagine.

The men were arguing now. When they glanced her way it was with revulsion instead of lust. She stood, naked and bleeding as they fought. One of them snatched a gun and held it to her head, yelling at the others. She closed her eyes and tried to be calm so she could say her goodbyes but the trigger was never pulled. Instead, another soldier approached her holding out a thin, gray blanket. It was the soldier she had seen with the shiisaa last night.

His face was blank where the other soldiers were overcome with emotions. He simply offered the blanket. She took it and their eyes met, but if he recognized her he didn't show it. She wrapped the scratchy wool around her shoulders, grateful to hide herself. She hoped the blanket, the color of shadow, could make her invisible. She looked for the quiet soldier but he had vanished.

A decision seemed to have been made and one of the soldiers approached her with some rope. Roughly, he wrapped it around her shoulders and arms, still wrapped in the blanket, and knotted it. He tied that to their small, iron stove. One of them gestured to her legs sticking out from under the blanket. The blood had formed sticky rivulets that attracted sand. The message was clear: her new femininity was disgusting. Kaori was both humiliated and grateful, but most of all afraid.

Thirteen

Shigeko, Zamami Island: The Dragon Comes

Shigeko's family sat silent in the dying glow of dinner's fire. Usually this was a time of cozy connectedness. Tonight, the dark wasn't so friendly. Chiga was the only one able to sleep. His breathing grew soft and deep within minutes. Her parents sat awake and silent for hours.

Shigeko was unable to sleep either. She lay wide awake with her eyes closed. She hoped by feigning sleep she might coax it forth. She had just started to drift when the sound of her parents moving brought her back to alertness. Quietly, they snuck out of the house to the back garden. She could hear them murmuring. Shigeko slipped out of bed and crept to the open door to listen.

"Will the American's come?" Mother's voice was tight and brittle.

"They can try." Her father's voice was louder, bolder but it sounded too animated. He was trying hard to sound nonchalant. "We have hundreds of Shinyo waiting. The suicide boats are hidden all over the island. The Americans will get an unpleasant surprise if they venture too close."

"But what if the boats can't stop them? What if they make it here?"

"They will also have planes to blow up the enemy ships, but we won't be here. We will be safe in the shelters while the Japanese soldiers protect us."

Shigeko's mother murmured something soft and inaudible. Father replied, equally soft. Mother's answer was to begin crying.

"It is for honor," he said. "It is a gift to protect our children. Could you ever rest if our Shigeko was used like the girls in that sex house?"

"Can we ever rest if we blow our children to pieces?" The reply was a crisp snap in the drowsy night. It brought a cool clarity.

Shigeko's father replied, too low for Shigeko to hear and then suddenly her mother stood up.

"I won't be the one to pull the cord and I will hurt anyone else who tries." Her voice was venomous. "I apologize. I am too weak to kill my own children."

Shigeko's father spoke again, but her mother was walking toward the house, her posture stiff and unyielding. Shigeko had just enough time to scramble back into the bed. She tried to control her breathing and look asleep but her mother wasn't fooled. She came to her and knelt down at Shigeko's side.

"You shouldn't have heard that. You should not have to grow up so fast with so many burdens."

Without another word, Mother lay down beside her. The warmth of her mother finally calmed Shigeko and lulled her to sleep with a lullaby of breath.

Morning came in bright. Up so late the night before, Shigeko was tired. She remembered the conversation in the garden and sat up, tossing Chiga's arm off of her in the process. He rolled over and continued to sleep.

Her mother was already awake, sitting by the cold stove. She put a finger to her lips when she saw Shigeko awake. Shigeko slid out of bed quietly. Her mother took a small bundle out of their iced box and motioned for her to follow. They went to the garden and sat in the same places her parents had sat in the dark just hours before.

Without a word, her mother unwrapped the leftover slices of fried Spam from the morning before. It felt like a lifetime ago. Silently, they ate cold slices of canned meat with their fingers, relishing the silence and the companionship. When the last slice was gone, broken in half to share between them, they remained sitting.

The Sagari-bana blossoms still scented the cool morning air. The birds were in full chorus as if by the sheer ferocity of their song they could drive all the foreign invaders away. The morning looked untouched. There was no smell of heated metal and oil. Shigeko heard no shouts of the soldiers. The soldiers they were forced to house hadn't returned the night before, so they had their house to themselves again.

The light reached across the tops of the trees, making the air shimmer with the early heat. Shigeko stood up, wiped her greasy fingers on the wet leaves and stretched. Sleep had been light, but the bright morning was doing a lot to lift her spirits. Her mother sighed with satisfaction and picked up the bucket hanging from a peg on the house, preparing to begin their morning chores.

Then, streaking across the sky like invisible dragons, came the sirens.

Fourteen

Yuki, South Okinawa: Alone

Yuki cursed at herself for taking time to save the baby. Now she had lost her own mother, but there was no time for second guesses. There was no time to wish her family had spent less time butchering the goat meat they would have no time to eat. There was no time for regret. With strange soldier voices bouncing through the brush, she needed to run. Yuki scanned the dark, looking for a miracle.

"Please, show me what to do."

Her words were directed inward, to whatever spirits might help, to her shiisaa. Yuki didn't know many things, but she believed the two little guardians were real. Her grandmother had made them to protect her and they always had. Sometimes Yuki felt her grandmother's presence adding volume, texture and depth to what had just been a nudge in her mind before. It was toward this presence she now directed her plea.

"Show me where to hide."

Everyone else was already scattered. While she could still hear people running in the distance ahead, she was alone. She tried to follow the sounds of cursing, branches cracking and grunts when someone fell. The undergrowth was dense off the road. It was good for hiding in the dark. It was good for slowing down the soldiers coming behind. Yuki hoped they would stick to the road.

Instinctively, Yuki followed the path of least resistance where the trees thinned. Branches whipped her face as she fled. As she ran, she prayed that her family had found safety. Every time she heard the guns go off, she prayed that it wasn't them. In her mind, she kept seeing the bundle of bloody goat meat. *Please don't let that be Shoji. Please don't let that be Mama.* She was angry at her father vanishing at a time like this.

Suddenly, she burst out of the thick trees to tumble into a stream. More gunfire. Through the darkness, flashes of light sparkled in the trees. It was at a distance, but not distant enough. She needed to hide. She forced the panic away and closed her eyes. Yuki felt her mind go flat and smooth like sand before it expanded to encompass her surroundings. A voice in her mind, the male shiisaa: *There.*

She opened her eyes, turning, looking around for something to save her. Then she saw it.

At the edge of the river, half in shadow, a rocky outcropping peeked out from beneath rotting trunks. Trees had collapsed into a rough shelter, giving their lives at some point in the past to save Yuki now. She sprinted, no concern for the noise she made as she splashed, racing to outrun the sound of gunfire, and dove into the tangled pile of deadwood.

Beneath the overhanging, Yuki started digging herself a shallow den in the soft earth. It was deep enough to hide her if she covered herself with more soil. She wondered if she might be digging her own grave but pushed that out of her thoughts. The soldiers were coming and she needed to disappear into the island. Once she was nearly covered in dirt she pulled dead leaves and twigs up to hide her face.

She thanked the shiisaa for guiding her to this place. She thought of Shoji and Mama and sent prayers and desperate pleas for their safety. More gunfire sounded, so close to her she almost bolted from her hiding place. Someone was pleading, harsh foreign voices cursed and then the shots cut the cries short.

She groped until she found her shiisaa and squeezed them until they bit into her palms. The hard clay guardians would keep her safe. She had to believe in them. They would protect her family. They would protect her friends. Yuki didn't understand why the soldiers had come to her home or what they wanted. She could only pray for them to leave.

Eventually, the voices and the sound of guns faded. It took much longer for Yuki's heart to stop pounding against her ribs, beating her lungs to be free. She lay still in the gathering quiet. It was too quiet. The animals had fled. No birdsong broke the hush; even the waves seemed to be holding their breath. All lay silent in the humid night, listening with Yuki until she noticed the graying light.

Fifteen

Kaori, North Okinawa: Common Ground

Many of the soldiers left the hut after that. She was no longer interesting. At one point Kaori heard more gunfire followed by the mama pig and her piglets squealing. Then the squealing stopped. Kaori's terror and humiliation simmered into icy rage. Now that she had seen her enemy, she knew they were just men. Terrible, cruel men but still men. They could be hurt as much as she could.

As she lay sweating in the blanket, she began to call on all the spirits of the island. She called to her own spirit voice. She even called to the shiisaa in the grotto. She didn't mind dying if it meant these men would be gone as well.

At some point the chaos subsided. Kaori could see a bonfire through the cracks in the wall outside and she smelled meat cooking. The soldier that gave her the blanket came back in, bringing her a metal plate of roasted meat. He untied the ropes so she could use her hands. Kaori shoveled the meat into her mouth. She was starving. The soldier pulled a folded leather envelope from his shirt and showed a photo of a girl. Kaori studied it as she ate.

She looked to be about Kaori's age. This girl had pale hair and wore a long skirt that showed her calves. She had short socks and stiff looking shoes. She was carefully posed and smiling with all her teeth. Behind her was a wall covered in more photos and a tall table with flowers on it. There was no color, but Kaori could imagine what the different smells were like in this other place. The photograph was important to this soldier. Kaori wondered if he had lost this girl like she had lost her brother. She wondered what spirits he had in his land.

He said many things Kaori didn't understand. When she finished eating he put the photo away. He neglected to tie her hands back up. As he left he stood in the door and said many more things Kaori didn't understand but the message was clear. He was not like the others. He didn't want to be like the others. He didn't want to be here at all. Then he left, closing the door behind him.

All the noise outside had calmed down. After a few minutes Kaori dared to peek through a crack in the door. The men had built a large fire across the clearing. Tossed to the side were the bodies of her pigs. One had been hacked apart with a machete, parts of which were hanging in the fire on metal sticks and chains. The rest of the meat would be spoiled by tomorrow. The men lay around the fire on rough gray blankets, like the one that covered her, talking among themselves.

Kaori knew she must be quick. She turned away and found her mother's rag box. She fixed them as her mother had shown her. Quietly, she rummaged through the baskets, a thief in her own home, piling up food to take along with a small bundle of clothes she had collected. She remembered the gift for the shiisaa and thought of a small, silk square her mother saved in a wooden box. This had a perfume in it, and she would offer it to the shiisaa. She hoped it was an appropriate gift.

Next to the stove she found her mother's small iron cleaver and she kept that in her hand. She knew how to sever tendons and separate bones. She imagined these soldiers would come apart the same as the pigs and poultry. Once she had everything she could think of packed and ready, she pulled the blanket loosely over herself, sat down and waited for all the voices to go quiet. It struck her that she was now a woman. Given her current situation, she wondered how long that would last.

When all the men were silent, Kaori crept back to the door and opened it just enough to see through. Most of the men lay in the open, scattered across the clearing near the fire. There were a few tents but everything was still. Kaori clutched her cleaver and carefully started opening the door. She looked out at the soldiers, watching for movement from any of them. Movement did catch her eye, but it was not from the soldiers.

Against the tree line, the shiisaa stepped clear of the shadows and into the firelight. It walked among the men without fear. There was a slow, easy air about the beast. Kaori caught her breath and stepped carefully back into the house. She closed the door, latched it and clutched the small cleaver to her chest, calling out to all her heavenly and spiritual patrons to come protect her now.

There was no sound for many minutes and Kaori started to think she had imagined everything. She risked looking through the door again and there it was, standing still in the middle of the camp of men. As Kaori watched, one of the men rolled over, caught sight of the large animal that had suddenly appeared in the middle of their camp. Slowly, the shiisaa lifted a massive paw. The soldier screamed and then the paw came down and shattered his skull.

The camp erupted. Soldiers rolled off their blankets and piled out of the tents. Gunfire, screams and bodies filled the air. The shiisaa was ruthless. Kaori couldn't look away. As much as she hated these men she wondered if she were next. She couldn't be anything but horrified to see them torn apart, bloody bones protruding from shredded flesh.

One of the soldiers ran for her tiny house, intending to take shelter. The shiisaa caught up with him in a single, massive leap. The soldier fell and squeezed his gun, spraying bullets and blood all around him. Kaori gasped as a sharp sting caught her in the leg. There was now a wound in her thigh. Kaori was bleeding for the second time in a night.

She slid to the ground, shaking. Her leg didn't hurt, but her stomach had gone sick. She vomited there, scooting back to stay out of the mess. When she was empty she couldn't move. She had been shot. She had never known anyone to be shot but she knew people died when they were shot. Silently, Kaori cried. When her tears were also empty, she lay still on the dirt floor. That's when she realized the screams were finished and everything was silent.

There were no more screams, no cries for help, no snapping of bones. The fire crackled. An owl hooted three times. There was no other sound. Kaori was weak, but not dying. She pushed herself up. Now her leg hurt. It was soaked in blood but it was no longer flowing free. She pulled apart her bundle until she found one of the strips of rag and wrapped it around her leg, tightly binding the wounds. She didn't know what to do with this bullet hole or who might be left on the island who could help her, but that was a problem for later.

Through the small windows, she could see the sky was beginning to lighten. Dawn approached. She drug herself back to the door. The sun was just peeking over the ocean's edge, casting light upon a scene of carnage. Nothing moved. Cautiously, Kaori pulled herself to her feet, gathered her bundle and opened the door.

Bodies were everywhere. As her eyes adjusted, she realized not all the red was blood and gore. Hibiscus blossoms were scattered across among piles of disemboweled torsos. Headless corpses were propped upright with beautiful leis hung around their necks. The heads were decorated with flowers in the eye's empty sockets, the reds blending together so seamlessly it was hard to distinguish flora from fauna. The flowers melted across flesh, stems blending with entrails. Kaori vomited again.

When she was finished, she steeled her nerves and hobbled as well as she could among the bodies. A calm settled over. These soldiers had come to destroy her island. They wanted to destroy her. The island had protected itself—and protected her. She couldn't put much weight on her right leg or bend it much, but she managed. As she passed one of the bodies she saw it was the soldier that had given her the blanket.

His chest was soaked in blood and it pooled around him. He was gasping in pain, rhythmically, lips pulled back. He saw her and started speaking fast and breathless but Kaori couldn't understand a word. His lips were cracked. She signaled to him she would bring water but he protested, waving his hands. He fumbled in the jacket next to him and found the leather envelope. Shaking, he removed the photo of the girl he had shown her and held it out to Kaori. Tears, blood and sweat covered his face.

"Mary… Mary…"

Kaori reached out and took the photograph. She didn't know what he wanted, but she nodded. He nodded back to her, satisfied, and collapsed back onto the mat with a final exhale. He would never be thirsty again.

He was her enemy. His war had settled on her island to fight someone else's war. To his people, her home was just a strategic location. They had not asked permission. They had assumed and consumed. But he had been a human as well. He couldn't be blamed for the sins of his people, could he?

Kaori picked up one of the scattered hibiscus blooms. She left it resting on his chest, the red of her home bleeding into his blood. This war that belonged to neither of them was out of both of their hands. The suffering and loss were mutual. She had somewhere to be.

Sixteen

Shigeko, Zamami Island: Enemies Among Us

The breakfast turned to clay in Shigeko's stomach and she had a sudden urge to use the outhouse. There was no time for that. Mother dropped the bucket and rushed into the house, pulling Shigeko with her. She piled belongings into Shigeko's arms and hung bags across her neck. Still packed from the night before, potatoes, bitter melons and tins of sardines weighed her down.

Chiga was tumbled from bed without ceremony. He had slept with the male shiisaa in his sweaty fist all night. Now the little clay guardian rolled across the floor. Shigeko struggled beneath her burdens to retrieve it. This would be a good time to return the guardian to her own pocket, but Chiga was already reaching out in desperation. Shigeko gave him half of the greatest treasure she owned, chiding him to be more careful.

Out of the corner of her eye she saw her father take the grenade from the shelf and tuck it carefully away. Mother noticed and stared at him coldly before pointedly turning her back to him. She busied herself with rolling their bedding to one side without shaking it.

"We will probably walk half the way and they will tell us to come home again," he said, as if it were an excuse for tucking death into the front of his shirt. No one in his house said a word, but a reply came to his statement from outside.

"The enemy has landed! Americans are here! Run to shelters!"

The cry was quickly taken up by other voices and panic escalated. All the nightmare stories they had been told about the tall, white demons were coming true. Their boots were on the island. Shigeko could feel the vibrations of their oversize feet pounding into her beaches. A sudden explosion tore through the air not so far off and a plume of darkness wormed its way into the sky.

"We must hurry to the shelter!"

Her father scooped them all out the door, Shigeko's mother still fussing over the scattered bedding.

"No time, no time!"

And suddenly, they were hurrying through a crowd of friends and neighbors turned strangers with fear.

"Go! Go!"

Panicked yells came from every direction. Shigeko clung to her father who was steering her mother and Chiga through the crowd. Another explosion ripped through the morning. Shigeko looked up to see several plumes of smoke winding their way toward the sun like fingers smearing charcoal across blue silk.

"Where are we going?"

Shigeko thought her voice was lost in the noise around her and didn't expect an answer, but her father heard.

"A bunker. The principal of Kokumin School is going there. We will have friends there."

Before her father had been enlisted to dig bunkers, he had been a caretaker at this school, so he was familiar with the faculty. It would be a well supplied and safe bunker to wait in. Shigeko hoped she would see friends there.

In the rush, someone knocked into her mother so hard she almost dropped Chiga who was clinging to her back like a monkey. Her father had rigged up a cloth strip to make a sort of carrying harness. Chiga looked scared, hanging on like that. He'd wanted to walk himself but her parents had ignored his protests as if he were a baby again. His hands were twisted in her mother's hair. Shigeko knew it had to be painful, but her mother didn't seem to notice.

"We are nearly there!"

Her father shoved someone so they fell and then rushed on, shouting apologies. Shigeko barely caught a glimpse of them as they hurried by. It was a face she recognized but couldn't place. Terror was a veil falling over them all. Her family, all of them, were transforming into stampeding animals. A tremble began to quiver up in her head and she thought she might start crying. The world had taken on a shimmer. It was unreal, an illusion preparing to collapse. Chiga was crying openly now, but he was little. It was to be expected. Shigeko had to be brave for him.

She hadn't been to the school bunker, so she didn't know what to expect or how far it was. They ran madly through the woods for a few minutes, and then suddenly, they were there. All that could be seen was a thick wooden door cut right into a hill. It was almost unnoticeable, which she supposed was the point. Once inside, rough wooden boards lined a short hallway that led to a windowless room dug into the earth. There were woolen blankets to sit on, a shelf with some supplies and a big jar full of water covered in a cloth.

None of her friends were here, only school staff and their families. Shigeko felt awkward. Her father led them in with an air of pride. He pointed out sections of the wall he had built, told them where the water jar came from and how much money he had contributed to buying supplies. He spoke loudly, as if for the room. Shigeko wondered if he was justifying his family's place. It felt surreal.

"We can live in here for months," he told his family. "We will rest and play buusaa and cards while the war rages outside."

Shigeko sat on a blanket and looked around the dark room. It was dark, crowded and poorly lit. A blanket hung in one corner to provide some sort of privacy for the bucket on the other side. Flies were hovering around the makeshift toilet in anticipation. Right now the bunker door was open, letting in light, but once they closed it only a few candles and a smelly kerosene lantern would illuminate them… maybe for months. Shigeko felt the tremble that had begun in her head drop down to her stomach.

Shigeko's mother had sat down next to her and Chiga wriggled his way out of the makeshift harness. Now that they were out of the panicked crowds he had calmed down.

"Look Shigeko," he whispered. "Your shiisaa kept us safe."

He held out the male guardian Shigeko had let him take care of. She was glad it made him feel safe, but she wished she had it back to keep her safe as well.

A group of men stood near the open door, speaking in low voices. Something about them gave Shigeko shivers. She knew all of them by name, but today they were strangers to her. Her father stood among them. They were not the same easy going men she was familiar with. Instead, their movements were furtive and guilty. They kept glancing at their families, patting bulges hidden in shirt fronts. There was a small disagreement among them, but they kept it low. Her father reached into his shirt and pulled the grenade out and the men gathered around like school boys with contraband. Her father glanced at his own family, saw Shigeko watching him and turned away to hide what he held. Shigeko felt disappointment and shame for him.

After more discussion, the men pulled a low table near the door and each of them took grenades from hidden pockets and placed them in a line. The room got quiet as all eyes turned toward them.

"This is a dangerous table," said her father to the silent room. "We will guard it for safekeeping. This will only be used to protect us in case the enemy reaches us."

"Which they won't…!" said one of the teachers of the younger children.

"Right, which they won't. This is just in case, to preserve our honor."

A little girl began to cry. The other younger children joined her, giving in to the fear that pushed the wavering sunlight in the door back out. The group of men looked almost comical standing by their table of explosives, trying to look important as children cried all around them. Shigeko loved her father, but she wondered who the enemy really was.

Seventeen

Yuki, South Okinawa: One Last Drink

Y uki came out of a light doze with a start. There were no sounds except the water gently lapping against the creek bank. She crawled out of her hiding spot, listening. The woods were too quiet, making her soft movements sound like a stampede to her hearing. She crept forward with spider movements, trying to be silent.

Yuki waded in the stream until the water was to her knees, and drank deep from her cupped hands. The water filled her empty belly and refreshed her. She splashed it onto her face, washed her arms and neck clean of the grime that covered her.

"Hey, bring me some water."

Yuki choked on the mouthful of water she was guzzling and spit up into the shallow water. The voice came out of nowhere. It took her a few seconds to locate the speaker. A soldier was sitting half hidden in the bushes, his gun pointed at her.

"I said bring me some fresh water."

He poked the gun barrel in her direction with an unspoken warning.

Yuki realized the soldier was injured. Blood blossomed across his uniform like painted watercolor flowers. Sweat dripped from his face despite the relative coolness of the early morning. She bent down and cupped water in her hands to bring to him.

"No, *fresh* water. From up river."

He pointed the gun upstream. Yuki looked to where he pointed.

A woman's body lay across the small stream, partially blocking the flow. Undeterred, the water had found its way over and under her. A few snails had also found the woman, sliding along her fingers like rings. Yuki followed the flow of water with her gaze, tracking the blood that still mixed with the river to flow down and around her.

The tendrils of red dispersed by the time the water reached her, but now she couldn't untaste blood in the water she had drank, imagined or real. She threw the water in her hands away from her and backpedaled out of the stream. On her hands and knees, Yuki wretched and tried to spit the water out, but her greedy body hung on to it.

"Water now or you will join her."

Yuki wanted to run, but she was so close to the soldier she had no doubt his bullets would find her. She nodded and got to her feet. Wiping ropes of saliva off her chin, she moved toward the dead body in the river.

"Yes, that's it... before it reaches the body."

The soldier unclipped a metal cup and tossed it across the stream to Yuki. She flinched when it hit the ground in front of her. She looked up at the soldier, pleading. She did not want to go near that poor woman.

"Now! I need water." Again, he poked the gun at her as a threat. He looked weak but the weapon made up for it.

Yuki picked up the cup and moved toward the woman, sliding her feet in the damp soil. As she neared the body, she could see the woman was riddled with bullet holes. The flowing water washed over her, aside from the holes in the woman's gray and blue yukata, she might just be laying in the water to get cool. Yuki wondered where the woman had gotten all the bullet holes. She risked a glance at the soldier with the gun. He was still pointing it at her but his head was leaning against the tree. He was panting for breath with his eyes closed. He wasn't watching her. This was her chance to run.

She took off a few steps before he shot the ground in front of her feet. A small plume shot up just in front of her. She froze in place, her back waiting for more bullets to follow.

"Next time, no warning. Water."

Shaking, Yuki returned to the water's edge ahead of the woman where it had not yet reached her. She tried not to look but the woman was facing her now, staring sightless at her through the shallows. A tiny hand bobbed on the surface. A tiny body lay pressed to the woman's chest, a nursing babe that would never thirst again. The tiny cold lips nuzzled against her neck, the moving water playing a trick to animate the babe as if he still searched for his mother's breast from beneath the water. The soldier's voice snapped her back.

"Move!"

The soldier's voice was weak. If Yuki could put something between her and his gun, she was positive he wouldn't be able to chase her. His bullets would be faster, though, and there was no place she could hide. She bent to fill his cup with trembling hands. Tears coursed down her cheeks to join the brook.

Carefully, her hands spilling a good deal of the cup's contents as she walked, Yuki approached the soldier. His eyes burned as he watched her approach.

"Please don't kill me," she whispered.

He only watched her approach with no answer, his eyes fixated on the cup she carried. His lips were cracked and bleeding.

Yuki looked at the cup she was carrying and saw most of the water had spilled out already. Her shaking hands were to blame. In a few more feet the soldier would see he had brought him a nearly empty cup. There would be no place she could run. She would never see her family again. She hoped Shoji would be safe.

A thick metal rod came out of nowhere and smacked down on the soldier's forearms, knocking the gun out of his grip. A boy about her own age was on the other end of the rod, his eyes wide, his lips pulled back as if he were screaming with no sound. The boy gripped the metal rod with both hands and plunged it deep into the soldier's stomach, twisted and then pulled it free.

It was a harpoon, a razor triangle of metal on the other end. It ripped flesh as the boy pulled backward. Upon exiting, it snagged a decent amount of entrails to dangle from the ragged tear. The soldiers' screams turned into a gargle. The boy dropped the broken weapon and turned to Yuki.

She was too stunned to move, too terrified to scream, but the boy didn't advance. He held his hands up to her as if she was a scared animal, showing her his palms. The metal cup dropped from her hands, splashing her toes with the little water that remained.

Behind him, voices rang out. A man called and other voices answered before a scattering of machine gun fire burst through the trees not far from them. The staccato sounds spurred her to action. With no more hesitation, she sprinted away from the boy, the dying soldier and the dead woman in the water. She had no goal save to get away. She ran blindly through the forest until she exploded out of the tree line and onto a small beach. Someone was running behind her but she didn't turn to look. Whether it was the boy or the soldier didn't matter. Her focus was on escape as she sprinted toward the water.

Yuki charged into the gentle waves. From the corner of her eye she saw the boy was running with her. He was covered in sweat and blood. As soon as he was waist deep in the water he dove, vanishing beneath the waves. Yuki risked a look back.

Behind them, no soldiers followed. The beach was clear, barely touched by the morning sun. In the shadowy edge of the tree line Yuki could see the shadows of men. Yuki dove as well, beneath the surface, and swam away as fast as she could. When she surfaced, there was a good distance between her and the chaos. She bobbed in the dark water, watching until she was sure none of them were coming after her and then she swam to put distance between herself and the invaders, parallel to the beach.

Yuki had spent her whole life on the island, but she had never spent much time alone this far from home. She had never slept outside. She was disoriented. The moon was still out, a ghostly disc hanging in the pale blue sky. The shoreline was a blot of shadow once she was out of view. Finally, she swam to a rocky outcropping that jutted out from a bare scoop of beach with a flat, grassy expanse of beach grass and hid there among the rocks, hidden from the forest.

She was hungry and cold. Her clothes clung to her as she moved in the water but there was nothing she could do about it. She felt like the forests were watching her. In the distance she could hear the voices of soldiers still yelling but she had no way of knowing how many there were. Was that all of them, or were they spread out across the entire island, silent and waiting to kill all the people she knew?

Something moved beneath the waves toward her and she recognized the boy's brown body just in time to suppress a scream. He surfaced silently next to her, just his head, and looked past her to the trees.

Eighteen

Kaori, North Okinawa: Last Supper

Kaori didn't know how many soldiers were on her small island but she knew that had not been all of them. She could still feel them. Mechanical noises, toxic odors and metal clangs echoed regularly, but it was the island itself that let her know there was something wrong. The birds were quiet, the trees were still and the wandering breeze carried the scent of spoiled meat.

Kaori didn't want to meet any more soldiers, but she was no longer afraid. These strangers were made of vulnerable flesh just as she was. They had hearts, families… they felt pain. They were from a different place. She imagined their guiding spirits must have fled a long time ago leaving them with no directions. They were cruel, empty shells of people.

Kaori found a sturdy stick to help her navigate the uneven ground. Because of her wounded leg, her progress was almost as slow as the day before. Still cautious, she moved carefully but she felt less threatened. She decided the shiisaa wasn't there because of her, but because of these invaders. The island had sent him. Twice he had shown up when she needed intervention and neither time had he attacked her. It couldn't be a coincidence. The island had awakened the shiisaa to protect. She wasn't sure if he was a friend but she was convinced he was not her enemy. If she helped him protect, maybe he would return her brother.

Only once did Kaori duck and hide. A swarm of planes flew overhead low. Through the brush she could see the rising sun painted on the metallic skin. They flew the way she came and then passed her, heading to the open sea. Once the planes were past, she resumed her slow, painful hike.

When she finally reached the grove that led to the grotto, she allowed herself to rest. She thought of the girl who had run this way just the day before. That girl was scared, slipping in fallen fruit as she sped past the trees. She had become a woman overnight. Now she returned to the grove like a crone, slow and leaning on a stick.

This time, she felt safe in the grove. These trees were old friends she had known all her life. Her mother had played here as a girl. She knew this place. Above her, the grotto waited with the cool, healing waters but the grove was healing her as well.

She found a ripe mango, pierced the skin with her fingernail and slurped the sweet flesh through the skin. The flavor was intense, the best mango she had ever tasted. She had spent the night thinking she was going to die. She spent the morning walking through the dead. She still lived. Every moment after this was a gift.

When she was finished, she licked her fingers clean and lay back. The day was moving on and she wanted to savor these moments. The home she had always known was poisoned. Even from here she smelled the metallic burn. Poisoned, but she had never loved it more. She had taken it all for granted.

When the stars began to dot the sky, she stood up and made her way to the rocky path. Limping along slow and steady, she hoped she'd be able to cleanse her wound in the waters. She was covered in blood, hers and others. Being clean was also something she had taken for granted. Even though she was in the worst shape of her life, Kaori had never felt so blessed. She hoped she would always remember the moment, regardless of what waited just ahead.

As she reached the opening, she slowed even more. She listened carefully to the usual sounds of falling water for any noises of the shiisaa or her little brother. Her stick thunked against the stone loud. Other than her own shuffles, there was nothing unusual. She stepped into the grotto. The water reflected the night sky like a silver mirror. The hibiscus blooms remained. Kaori slid her little bundle off and began opening it.

The small bundles she unknotted and spread out on the rocks near the hidden cave opening. She laid out three bitter melons, two sweet potatoes and a broken taro root. She set down a jug of the liquor her father made. Finally, she unfolded the small square of silk. Kaori smelled it. The perfume mixed with the scent of her mother. It was something else she had taken for granted. She left the offerings there, hoping it would be enough to appease whoever she may have offended.

Painfully, she stripped out of her soiled clothes. She would help the shiisaa protect the island. She would trade herself for her baby brother. She sank into the silver pool, among the flowers. The relief was instant. Her abdomen and leg stopped throbbing. She sank beneath the water, scrubbing her scalp and finger combing through the tangles. For everything that had happened, Kaori felt overwhelmed by the beauty all around her.

Eventually she climbed out, dried herself and dressed in the fresh garments. Then she sat on the rocks to watch the cave entrance. The moon rose overhead, shining down into the narrow cleft. Her reflection shimmered in the pool. Where the light touched the falling water, the beams shattered and swirled like a school of minnows made of starlight. She had started to nod when she heard the voice she was waiting for.

"Kaori?"

She was instantly awake.

Nineteen

Shigeko, Zamami Island: Final Stand

Mothers hushed their babies. The older children soothed their siblings. The children without siblings withdrew into themselves. The men stood alone by the table, unwelcomed by their families. Wives avoided eye contact with them.

Another explosion sounded, closer. Bits of earth crumbled from the ceiling and a few of the smaller children squealed in panic. One of the women tore open a package of sweet brown sugar chunks and the smaller children were quickly soothed.

"It's okay," Chiga said out loud, addressing the room. "We have this shiisaa to protect us. As long as we stay calm, he will keep us safe." He held the little clay lion-dog up for everyone to see. "It's really my sister's but I'm taking care of him."

He looked so earnest and brave standing there alone as everyone around him was giving in to fear. Any respect Shigeko had lost for her father transferred to Chiga at that moment. Her little brother was sure to grow up to be a leader. Another explosion shook the room and Chiga said nothing. He just held the shiisaa up high and it seemed to work some magic.

On the other side of the room a few women were talking in low, agitated voices, oblivious to Chiga's pep talk. Shigeko could catch snippets of what they said. They were discussing the painful and humiliating ways the enemy would kill their children. "Our daughters will be used like animals." She pulled her daughter closer, a girl maybe a year younger than Chiga who was listening with wide eyes. The woman she spoke to only nodded, dabbing at her eyes.

Shigeko slipped her hand into her own pocket and gave the girl shiisaa she had kept a squeeze. She tried hard not to look at the low table that held all the grenades, but it was nearly impossible not to. They were like a horrible beacon. Then one of the men closed the door and cut off the light as another explosion shook them. Shigeko immediately longed for the sun.

Time evaporated along with the light. They sat in silence, waiting. Measurements like hours and minutes ceased to exist and those in the room began to count the passage of time by explosion. At one point, a nearby blast was followed by a man's screams. They all sat in the dark listening until a woman spoke.

"Open the door! Help him!"

"No! He may be a soldier. We can't risk it." In the dim light from the crack in the door, Shigeko could see a few of the men had stood up, blocking it.

"He is one of us, suffering. Help him!" Some of the women were getting agitated. The man could be heard crying not too far away. He spoke uchinaaguchi. He was an islander.

"Hear him? One of us! Open the door and save him."

The men looked threatened. They all stood now, forming a wall between the room and the door.

"Our duty is to protect our families. We will even protect our families from themselves, if needed."

The man's screaming was horrible and a few of the women were standing now, raising their voices. Other women stood up with them. It was becoming an argument. Another explosion, the closest yet, ended it. The explosion was close enough to rock the little room dug in the earth. On the bench, the grenades rattled together from the impact. The jingle of metal on metal set Shigeko's nerves on edge. Outside, there was the sound of machine gun fire and the screaming man was suddenly silent. Shigeko felt like a prisoner among her own people.

Strange voices echoed nearby, but they were not the voices of the Japanese. Flat, harsh and loud, these voices traveled too far. They forced themselves onto the island quiet, rupturing it. Shigeko could feel the land recoiling from the sounds. More machine gun fire rang out and then laughter. Inside the bunker there was silence broken only by the pounding of hearts.

The voices came closer. One of the women stood.

"They are coming…" she hissed. "They will rape our children in front of us. You must use the grenades."

Shigeko was horrified. She didn't want to die. Maybe the soldiers wouldn't see the small door cut in the hill. If this woman would be quiet, maybe they would pass by. One of the men was trying to calm her down but her hysteria was ramping up. In the dim light Shigeko could see her skin gleaming and covered in sweat. Drops were running down her face, plastering her hair to her skin. The woman was breathing too fast.

"Be quiet!" One of the men grabbed her by the shoulders and shook her to snap her from her fear, but it only made things worse.

"Kill us! Save us from the Demons! Don't let them have us!"

Over the woman's mounting hysteria, Shigeko could hear the soldiers turning their direction. She couldn't understand their words but the meaning was clear. They had heard something. They were coming to investigate. Shigeko stood up, terrified, and ran to the hysterical woman to calm her down. The soldiers would move on if this woman would be quiet.

"Make her be quiet!"

"You must kill us!"

"The soldiers hear us!"

One of the men grabbed a grenade at the ready and opened the shelter door, ready to lob the explosive at the approaching Americans. Hysteria was gripping other women and they were joining in with the pleas for the men to kill them. One of the women rushed forward, shoved Shigeko to one side and grabbed a grenade off the table. Shigeko tripped and fell backwards. She watched as the woman pulled the black cord that was attached to the fork. The grenade was going to explode. The room went silent as they all stared at the woman, her hands trembling, a bit of black string dangling from her shaking fingers.

"I don't want to die!" Shigeko shrieked at her. Anger took over her fear. It was about to be her birthday. This was not her war, not her death. None of this was fair.

The woman looked at Shigeko, her face twisted into terror, and then she threw the grenade from them and across the room. Shigeko saw it arc in the candle light. As if pulled forward on a string, it flew straight to her mother and Chiga. She saw their faces, saw the light shining in their eyes. Chiga was standing straight, serious, watching the grenade fly to him. His arm was held up high, holding the shiisaa. Shigeko screamed and her world exploded.

The bomb's roar was so loud it chased all the sound from the world. She only heard ringing. She lay on her back, weighed down by a man in blue and gray weave. His shoulder was across her face. She studied the weave of his shirt, trying to remember who had worn that pattern. Where had she seen it... Then she was trying to push the body off. *Father... Chiga... mother...*

Twenty

Yuki, South Okinawa: A Ruined Pair

"Did they follow?"

Yuki shook her head no. He was from the island, though she didn't know him. He wore a short jacket and pants. He had killed a soldier all by himself. He had saved her. He scrubbed his hands and fingernails in the water. The blood on him became a smudge in the water that quickly dispersed. He looked up at Yuki.

"Are you okay?" he asked.

She nodded. She had watched him kill a man twice his size or more. She felt afraid of this boy, but also grateful and a little safer.

"I can't believe you killed him."

The boy looked hurt. He looked at his hands under the water, clean now and all traces of blood washed away. Yuki wondered if he would always see his hands that way from now on. He might have been thinking the same way. He turned away from her, and she wondered if she had insulted him. She felt awkward.

"Sorry, I didn't mean it like that. I was rude. You saved me."

Then she thought of Shoji. Was he crying right now? All the shots she heard as they fled through the darkness, her Mama alone trying to run with a monkey boy clinging to her. Her father gone as well. Were they alive? Did they lay in a river somewhere too? The tiny cold baby, little blue fist waving in the current…

Then she was crying. Sobs tore out of her in gasps. She couldn't breathe. The boy wrapped his arms around her. The wet cloth of his jacket felt good against her hot face. His body shook and she thought he might be crying with her. They clung to each other while the sun grew hot around them and the sky brightened into full day. They were two strangers lost together in it.

When they both grew still, Yuki felt awkward again. She had never been held by any male other than her father or Shoji. She cleared her throat and pulled back, and he let her go. His eyes were red and swollen. He splashed sea water on his face and rubbed them. Yuki did the same.

"What do we do now?" she asked.

His eyes were on the shore. The sounds of gunfire had ceased and the normal island noises had returned for now. Carefully, he moved around the rocky outcropping for a better view. Finally, he spoke.

"My home isn't far from here. We can see if it's safe to go there. At least we can find some food there."

As if on cue, Yuki's stomach gave a loud gurgle that wasn't muffled at all by the water. She hadn't eaten anything but a lump of the sugar candy yesterday and she was instantly ravenous.

"I'll take that as a yes," he said and Yuki giggled. There were many things to be afraid of, but at least, at this moment, he wasn't one of them. Together, they swam to shore.

This part of the island felt deserted now. There were no soldiers. There were no people either. The air felt strange—too quiet, with unfamiliar smells traveling in the breeze. The forest was broken with the splintered trunks of trees twisting up to the sky. As they walked they found they had a lot in common.

His name was Kana. He had lived with his parents and a younger sibling the same age as Shoji, but a little sister named Kame. He had been separated from his parents in the panic just like Yuki had. He had been hiding in a tree top not far from where she had chosen to bury herself. When he had seen the soldier about to shoot her he had to act. As they spoke a sense of normalcy returned with the morning.

Then they found a body.

Yuki heard the flies first. Dozens of them swarming around just off the animal track they were following. She'd never heard so many flies in one place before. She stopped. Kana had been in the middle of explaining how to make a spear. He turned to see why she stopped and noticed the flies as well.

They didn't smell anything as they moved forward to see. The insects bounced off their faces. They saw the feet first. A man, one sandal lost. He was wearing a gray kimono with a blue checked weave. Yuki's mother could make that pattern. His back was soaked in blood. There were holes punched through the fabric. The flies were going in and out of the holes, laying their eggs. His flesh was beginning to turn bad.

Without a word, the two children walked backwards, unwilling to turn their backs on the corpse. When they got back to the animal track they walked silently, in single file, until they got to a stand of houses that was Kana's village. Instead of going to the front they walked behind all the buildings and entered his house from the back. It was similar to Yuki's own house and in a similar disarray. Kana's family had hurried to leave just as rushed. Yuki wondered if all the houses were like this—spilled baskets, bedding left out and clothes strewn across the floor.

Without a word, Yuki started picking things up and putting them away. Kana built a fire in the little stove, got water, and started it boiling. Yuki went to the garden and found cabbage and purple sweet potatoes. She cut everything up, dropping it in the water to boil into a vegetable broth. They worked in silence.

When done, she served it into bowls just like she had for her own family so many times. Kana's house looked normal with everything put in place. They sat on the floor together and sipped. They had been working for a few hours. When they were finished, Yuki put a lid on the pot so they could finish it later and washed the two bowls. Finally, Kana spoke.

"I knew him."

Yuki didn't have to ask who he meant. They hadn't been alone in the house. The spirit of the dead man was with them. Yuki saw his body superimposed over the small chores she busied herself with. She kept wondering about things that didn't matter. Could the man's kimono be patched? Where was his other sandal? How sad that he lost it.

She tried to shake these thoughts out of her head with busy work but they were lodged too snugly. The man was dead and she didn't even know him, but what about her own father, her mother, Shoji… were they the same somewhere, covered in flies and missing one sandal?

"Was he…? Who was he?"

"His name was Toshio. He lived alone. His wife passed away when I was still little."

Yuki didn't know what to say, so she said nothing. A single fly buzzed in the room and they both pretended not to notice when it landed on Yuki's cheek. She refused to flinch. Kana stood up without saying anything more and went to the back where he sat in the garden on a stump. Yuki stayed in the house. A full stomach overtook her and she fell asleep sitting up, leaning against a wall.

When Kana gently shook her awake, it was evening and the sun was going down. Other than the sounds of a vehicle somewhere and some more gunfire, the day had been silent. He had been busy while she slept. He had packed some of the remaining food in case they had to flee. For dinner, they each had the rest of the vegetable broth. Yuki felt much better.

Kana suggested they stay there, in his house, and wait for his parents to return. They had plenty of food, he reasoned, and they could wait in reasonable safety and comfort. If soldiers came they could easily escape into the woods that backed up to his house. He assured Yuki he knew the woods well and even had a hidden place they could escape to if needed. If by the third day no one had returned, they would go look for their families together. Neither of them mentioned him again, but they both thought of Toshio lying in the grass with one sandal, a ruined pair.

Twenty-One

Kaori, North Okinawa: Finding a Hiro

"Hiro?"

The only answer was the water splashing on stone. Enough time went by that Kaori thought she must have imagined the voice. She was disappointed. And then, Hiro's voice again.

"Don't be scared."

"Hiro! I'm not scared. I came to take you home. Can you come home with me? Can I take you home?"

There was another long pause but Kaori knew she wasn't dreaming. She waited.

"We can't go home. The soldiers are angry."

"We can make a new home. We can get a boat and follow…"

"I can't leave the island with the soldiers here."

Hiro wasn't speaking like her baby brother. His speech was slow and even, not the little boy she remembered.

"How do you know about all the soldiers, Hiro? Can you see them?"

Again, there was a long silence. Kaori felt like the grotto was getting cold. Nothing moved in the cave.

"When the soldiers are gone I can come back. Don't be scared."

"I'm not scared. Hiro, is the shiisaa there? If he lets you go I'll take your place."

"Kaori…" Silence.

"Yes?"

"Don't be scared…"

Kaori opened her mouth to assure Hiro she wasn't but something finally moved behind the fall. Sizable, like the rock walls had detached, it moved toward her silent except the soft foot pads against the stone floor.

In spite of her promise, Kaori lurched to her feet, ready to run.

"Kaori…" It was Hiro's voice, but not as a little boy. Something was pushing through the water. It bent to clear the cave. Tall, broad… a coppery lion dog emerged from the water before her eyes. The beast shook its head, flinging water from its mane.

"Hiro…" Kaori's voice was now a breathless squeak.

"Don't be afraid."

It was Hiro speaking, Hiro's strange grown up voice, but the words were coming from the massive shiisaa pushing through the water. It stood up on all fours. If it stood on hind legs it might have reached the top of the grotto. It could easily block her from running back down the cut stone path if she tried, even if both her legs were whole.

The moonlight shone down on his face as it cleared the waterfall and stretched to full height. His black eyes were like twin orbs of squid ink. The stars caught in the reflection, swirling as he watched for her reaction. Kaori couldn't move. She couldn't speak. She couldn't feel. Around them, everything receded as her brain tried to work out the situation.

"I'm taller than you now." There was a hint of a smile in his voice, the little brother's too-serious voice that came from a shiisaa mouth.

Kaori's own mouth worked to speak, opening and closing like a fish. Finally, she got a word out. It was a whisper, hopeful and terrified.

"Hiro?"

The shiisaa nodded.

"Are you afraid?"

Slowly, she shook her head no. They both knew she was lying, but they also both knew that's what big sisters did when things were too scary. Trying not to bend her damaged leg, Kaori sat back down. Hiro-shiisaa sat down too, in the water. His hindquarters stuck out above the surface like an island.

They stared at each other while Kaori tried to decide what to do.

"So… *you* are the shiisaa?"

He shook his head. "There's no shiisaa. It's just me. It's been me all this time."

"Where have you been? Where did the spirits take you?"

A paw waved toward the cut stone path and Kaori flinched. "I've been in the grove. No one took me there. I've always been there."

"You weren't always in the grove. You used to live with me. In our house—"

"Yes! I dreamed about that place. The house and the field of bodies around it. It was different from when I dreamed it before. There was Mama."

"Yes, Hiro. Your mama… our mama. She misses you. Look!" Kaori groped around in the offerings, knocking vegetables off the stone so they plunked into the pool. Her fingers found the small square of silk. "This—this belonged to her. I brought it for you."

She held the little cloth out. The moonlight gleamed on the smooth fibers. His massive paw reached out and snagged it with an obsidian claw set in shimmering red velvet. Scents of turmeric and Sagari-bana wafted toward her. She wanted to bury her face in his fur. He was changed, but he was still Hiro.

"Hiro… what happened?"

He said nothing, holding the precious silk square aloft and looking at the color in the moonlight. He brought it to his face and inhaled. It sounded a little like the bamboo flutes they used to make.

"This smells like her…"

"Yes! That smells like our mother. And she misses you."

Again, he inhaled with a flute note, long.

"I miss you."

Just breathing. He had grown motionless, a copper sculpture in the middle of the pool, a small square of silk pinned to the paw.

"I want to go back."

"I want you to come back. I'm so sorry for giving you away…" All of this.

All of this could be made right.

"You didn't give me away, I wasn't yours to give. The island needed me. It asked, and I said yes."

Kaori shook her head. "No, what I did was wrong…"

"Kaori, the island asked if I would protect and I said yes. And I can't come back until. I promised."

"Until what?"

"Until they're gone."

"The soldiers?"

"The soldiers. For now."

"If the soldiers go you can come back?"

Hiro-shiisaa didn't answer. He sat back in the water and was still for a long time. Kaori thought maybe he hadn't understood.

"If we…"

"Hush." Hiro sounded more like the spoiled brother she remembered then. "I'm asking."

Confused, Kaori complied. Her mind was whirring as she tried to sort out what was happening. *If we get rid of the soldiers, Hiro can come home.* She remembered the field of corpses strewn with flowers and felt sick. *Whatever it takes. I have to fix this.*

Finally, Hiro spoke.

"When I'm not needed, I can come back sometimes. But when I'm not needed I might also be sleeping."

Kaori didn't know what that meant, but it wasn't what mattered. What mattered was there was a chance for Hiro to return. In some way… compromise was a good start.

"What do I have to do?"

Kaori struggled to her feet, swaying slightly. She felt better than she had since she watched their parents go just days ago, but her head was too light. "I'm ready, Hiro."

Massive velvet paws stretched across the water to her, wrapping around her, gently cradling her. Hiro picked her up and she didn't protest.

"Rest first," said Hiro. "I'll ask what to do."

He laid Kaori in a hollow of smooth stone. Her head was full of bees and slow, honeyed thoughts.

"Ask who?" But she didn't listen for the answer. She found Hiro and she wasn't scared of the shiisaa. The fact that they were the same didn't matter right now. Kaori slept, dreamless, and was replenished.

Twenty-Two

Shigeko, Zamami Island: Another Broken Pair

She wriggled from under him. As he rolled off she caught sight of his face. It was bloodied and blind, fragments of metal embedded in his bone, slicing his nose off his face. The front of his shirt was soaked in blood. Then she recognized him.

"Father!"

Her voice came from far away. She didn't even recognize it. Her father couldn't see her. His eyes were missing, ruined cavities where they had once been. She looked away to where her mother and Chiga had been. The room was so bright, it blinded her.

The back of the bunker was missing. Shigeko could see the forest through the new opening. People were laying everywhere, tangled together. They had piled on top of each other like driftwood. She stumbled forward to see if she could help. A hand protruded, reaching for help. When she tugged it came free and she sat down hard, knocking her breath away. The hand had come loose with a length of forearm almost to the elbow, but there was nothing more. A human limb, broken and bleeding lay in her lap. Shigeko gasped, trying to catch her breath.

In the pile of bodies, she saw Chiga's face. He was still perfect, his sweaty little bangs stuck to his forehead. His eyes were closed. Shigeko pushed the arm away and crawled forward. She had to get her little brother out of here before he woke up. This would give him nightmares they would never hear the end of.

She reached him and put her hands under his armpits to pull him free. *Thank goodness, he doesn't look hurt.* Shigeko tugged, pushing her hip into the bodies that pinned him in and suddenly he slid free. Chiga slipped from the bodies, covered in blood from all the bodies, the other bodies. He would need a bath before the mess dried. *Thank goodness he's still asleep.*

She tried to pick him up but he was so slippery. His body felt formless, like mochi. She picked him up like she had done 100 times, but he slid out of her arms like an eel. She examined him where he lay, confused. He didn't look hurt. The blood was from the other bodies. None of it was his. She searched through his clothes looking for damage. Other than some bits of metal stuck in his skin, he seemed perfect. He just needed a bath before he woke up. All this blood would terrify him.

Chiga made a noise. She looked down at his perfect face. His eye lids were fluttering. She pulled his shirt over his strangely spongy body so he wouldn't see the blood. His eyes fluttered open but didn't look like him. Normally bright, his eyes were glazed over and dull. The whites were yellow, almost orange in this light.

"Chiga, it's going to be okay. I have you."

He seemed to focus on her for just a moment and he opened his mouth to say something. Blood gurgled out, and then he was coughing, choking on the blood that spilled from his mouth. His chest folded almost double and slipped from her arms. His eyes rolled back in his head, he gave a last choke and stopped breathing.

Suddenly, looking in from where the wall should be there was a giant. It was a man twice the size of her father with pink skin and yellow hair. A helmet shaped like a bowl hung from his hip. His bottom lip protruded. He looked at her, said something she couldn't understand and then turned his head to spit brown venom into the corner of the shelter. He held out his hand and took a step toward her.

Shigeko stood up and backed away. He said something else in his flat dialect and stepped toward her, holding his hands out like she was a scared dog. He was treating her like she wasn't human. He took another step and his boot crushed something. They both looked down. It was the male shiisaa, the one that Chiga held up as the grenade blew up her world. It was a warning. Shigeko heeded it.

She was out the open bunker door in a flash. There were soldiers scattered everywhere. They shouted at her and reached for her as she ran, but she was too fast. Like a rabbit, Shigeko darted among the men, evading and sprinting until she was past them all. She ran blind with no thoughts as to where she was headed until she found herself at the beach where she had watched Japanese soldiers hide a suicide boat a few days before. It was a lifetime ago.

The place where the boat was hidden looked undisturbed. The strange voices were yelling on the ridge above the beach. Shigeko had to hide. She ran to the small dugout place where she had seen them slide the boat, pushed her way through the tall, sharp grass and slipped in. She replaced the vegetation behind her.

The boat sat undisturbed, a plywood coffin waiting for a doomed pilot. About six meters long, there was a place in the back to steer. It was here that Shigeko climbed in and curled up. Hours ago she had been angry with her father for having a grenade. Now here she was, curled up on a boat loaded with explosives. None of that mattered now.

Laying on the boat floor, she looked up at the roof of the shallow cave. Chiga was gone. Her mother, so close to him when the grenade hit, was also probably gone. Her father—she remembered the blue and gray plaid that had fallen on her, probably protecting her from the blast. She didn't weep until she remembered her little male shiisaa beneath the soldier's heel, his giant boot crushing it. The shiisaa her babaan had made. Her girl guardian was alone forever now. Then she could let the tears flow silently until she fell into exhausted, dreamless sleep.

Twenty-Three

Yuki, South Okinawa: Enemy of My Enemy

The two of them went through the motions of housekeeping with few words between them and an abundance of tension. There was gunfire, the sound of vehicles and smells that didn't belong to this place. Once they heard flat, braying laughter rise up over the wind and they both froze, ready to grab the bundle Kana had put by the back door, but they heard nothing else. On the second morning a woman walked through the middle of the village. She shuffled like she was walking in her sleep.

Yuki softly called out. The woman stopped and turned to Yuki's voice. She had only one eye, the other was swollen shut. Her face was covered in blood and flies. Her mouth hung open, her teeth shattered. Her kimono was open, exposing her breasts.

Yuki ducked down so the woman wouldn't see her, too terrified. What she had mistaken for a woman was an angry yokai. Yuki held her shiisaa and prayed silently, hoping the demon would spare them and move on. Her prayers worked. When Kana came in from the back he said there was no one in the street.

That night they both woke to hear a woman screaming in the distance. They huddled together as the shrieks filled the empty space around them. Yuki thought of the yokai she had seen earlier. The screeching was an endless, unnatural tearing of the night. Sharp, staccato gunfire rang out and cut the breathless wail off. Yuki wondered if the ghost had found a victim, or became one.

Neither could sleep after that. They lay silent and wide awake. Since their first day in Kana's house, they had said very few words to each other. They moved silently, like ghosts themselves, nervous and twitchy. Kana acted like a stranger in his own house, as if he were an intruder.

The morning of the third day Kana mentioned that maybe they should leave and see if they could find their parents. Yuki wanted to stay. In spite of the fearful silence, the house felt safe compared to the explosions they heard in the distance. There was fresh water and food in Kana's house.

There were also distractions. Yuki had found a tiny hand loom and she had started making small patches with it. At first she unraveled rags for thread, carefully picking apart the fabric to salvage what she could. She absorbed herself in the task, occupying her mind to avoid thinking about anything else. Soon she had piles of tiny tapestries, colorful little patches waiting to repair something.

Kana had his own distraction. He spent most of the time in the back garden, turning the soil, pulling weeds, digging new furrows. Every day he brought in more vegetables than they could eat. Neither had much appetite after the first day. Yuki poured the leftovers in the back of the garden for animals. It was dull. Dull was a relief. Kana agreed they should stay for a few more days and wait. Neither wanted to find their families if…

Neither of them mentioned Toshio again.

They decided to remain while they could.

Once or twice, soldiers came marching through. When they did, the two teenagers hid in the house ready to flee. Japanese or American, it didn't matter where the invaders hailed from. None of them belonged on their island.

They had been in Kana's house for almost a week like this, actively engaged in not thinking about where their families were, or were not, content to slip into a trance of keeping busy.

At one point Yuki remembered how her own grandmother stayed so busy.

Had she also been trying not to think about death? Yuki thought of Toshio again. She thought of the yokai wandering through the village with a bloodied mouth. She thought of the babe and the mother staring at her from under water. Then she put all the thoughts away and bent over her work, picking threads from a perfectly good towel. She had run out of rags days ago.

A week grew into a new life. She and Kana would grow old here together. Their families might never return. She would pick all the threads in his house apart and then go hunt for more. This is what it meant to grow up. She pulled too hard and the thread she was working on snapped. Yuki felt very much like that thread. Her nerves were a pointless tangle trying to patch something unfixable.

Then the sky filled with planes.

They had been napping through the heat when the sound of aircraft sliced through their dreams with a distant whistle that had them both tumbling from the beds. The light was gray. Across the room, Kana was staring at the ceiling in confusion as the sound of planes filled the sky overhead. Yuki's heart started thudding in her chest. The fog of an impending headache crept around the edges of her vision, narrowing it.

Not now, please...

They were under attack again. This was not the time for her to be down with one of her crippling headaches. She had been sleeping fully dressed since she'd taken up housekeeping with Kana, and her shiisaa were never away from her. She pulled them out now and pressed them to her forehead.

Almost instantly, the shiisaa song washed over her mind, cooling it. Her vision cleared. She was going to make it. She slowed her breathing, matching it to the repetitive *aum*. Breathe in... breathe out... ignore the sound of an airborne army.

"Yuki..."

Kana's voice was small, tense. It reminded her of Shoji when he was scared.

Be safe, baby brother. Protect Mama...

"Yuki..."

She didn't open her eyes. She didn't want to. It was safer in a world where she couldn't see the next nightmare. If she didn't see it, maybe it would stay away. She tried to focus on the song but the noise from a hundred planes filled her head.

"Yuki…"

This time Kana's voice came from outside the house, louder. He had to raise his voice to be heard.

She opened her eyes.

He was just outside the door, staring up at the sky. Through the open door she could see lines of small planes in the same direction, hundreds of them in waves. They sounded like a swarm of giant wasps. It reminded Yuki of the sound of flies on a dead man who had lost one sandal. She went to stand beside Kana.

"It's the Japanese," he said. "They came to save us." His eyes were shining like he had a fever.

Twenty-Four

Kaori, North Okinawa: Seeking Balance

Kaori woke up as dawn was chasing the stars back into the velvet abyss. She sat up and scanned the small grotto for signs of Hiro. There were none. Standing up, Kaori suddenly realized how amazing she felt. Her leg was stiff but functional. There was little to no soreness. Her bullet wound was red and fresh but healed over. She was fully refreshed.

"Hiro?"

There was a stirring in the cave behind the waterfall.

"In here. I have to go this way."

With no questions, Kaori followed her little brother's voice through the curtain of water. Inside was the same grotto cave where she had sealed Hiro's future. Guilt knifed her heart.

"Hiro, I'm sorry," her voice cracked. "For everything."

"No." His voice came from around the bend where she had seen a shadow flit a lifetime ago. "The island would have no guardian now. Nothing is ever terrible or good. It's what we do with it that matters."

Kaori rounded the corner. The ceiling sloped up here, making a natural vaulted ceiling. Hiro-shiisaa was squatting at the end where the cave rounded another turn. When she came into view, he stood up.

"That's what the spirits told me."

He moved out of view around the bend.

"Hiro, wait!"

His footfalls echoed off the stone walls as the only reply as he moved away. Kaori was afraid to go on. The night before—finding Hiro, and what he was—seemed unreal. She'd been exhausted, maybe even hallucinating. With her head clear, her reasoning faculties took over. Was this really Hiro?

Her intuition assured her it was her brother. She thought of the soldiers being torn apart by the angry shiisaa—by Hiro? Nothing made sense except the voice in her gut telling her to trust, to listen. Kaori followed.

The passage was narrow but tall. At the end toward the grotto cave it was hewn from stone, like the hidden path to the falls. The further she went, the more the cave changed. The flat walls gave way to stones fit together on purpose, and then to stones that seemed more natural. The entire passage was short with light from either end dimly illuminating the entire passage. The sound of splashing water bounced off stone. Kaori was surprised she'd never explored past the grotto room. She'd been too afraid.

Hiro was waiting for her at the other end. They were in an opening above the grove. In all the times she had played here, Kaori had never noticed this place either. Another path was cut through the stone, making a smooth path to the wooded pocket below. Is this where Hiro had been the past year? Had he been this close? Or perhaps not that close—once the searches had stopped she had avoided this place.

"I think the gods made this." Hiro-shiisaa was sliding paws across the crudely carved stone floor.

Kaori didn't say anything in answer. The voices of the invaders traveled across the horizon to remind her how grim their situation was. The breeze had a metallic tang to it. She didn't know what lay ahead, but she was scared. She remembered the soldier who would not be returning to his sister. Who had wanted this war?

"What happens now, Hiro? Will you always be… like this?"

His fur rippled across his shoulders, Kaori supposed it could have been a shrug.

"I don't know, Kaori. Maybe after the soldiers go I can come back, and Mama can come back and I can meet the baby…" His voice trailed off.

"How did you know there was a baby?" Had Hiro been closer than she knew?

"The spirits told me. They said if we protect the island maybe there will be a way to return it all."

Protect the island. Kaori thought of the blood soaked sand around their house. The screams fleeing through the trees, the scattered pig corpses, a man leering at her, unzipping his pants. None of this was right, none of this should have come to her, Hiro or the island. They deserved none of it, but here it was. There was no other choice but to protect. She would not be the only one bleeding.

Kaori reached out and put her hand on his side. "I don't think I can kill anyone… like you… like last night."

"I don't want you to!" Hiro stood up. "I'm not always… me. The spirits do things. But I don't want to see it again." Hiro's voice was cracking and he sounded very much like the frightened little boy that had waited for her to come back. He reached out to her.

Kaori tried to hug her little brother but wound up jabbing herself on his claw instead. She yelped in surprise and pain, and then laughed. Hiro joined her. Their giggles had an edge of hysteria but it allowed them to release some of the fear. It frothed out of them, and when it subsided, Kaori felt much calmer.

"Let's do this, Hiro. Let's just do it before we get scared."

"Too late." Hiro's voice was small. If Kaori had her eyes closed she would have seen her baby brother again. Instead, he towered over her.

For a second, Kaori reconsidered. They could find a boat and join their parents. It didn't matter what Hiro looked like, he was still her brother. Nothing was final and no one could blame them. She could protect him this time.

Instead, she buried her face in his fur. "Just… trust the spirits. I will too. And if anything gets… too much… we will just leave the island. We're only children."

Not you, said her voice in her head. *You are a woman now.* Kaori had no time to think about the implications because it was time to move. Hiro was already halfway down the path.

While they walked, Kaori whispered breathless prayers to any gods, any spirits that might be able to help them now. *Please let Hiro be okay.* Now that she had him back, she couldn't lose him again.

Twenty-Five

Shigeko, Zamami Island: Home Visit

S higeko woke up to silence. She lay still trying to sort out her new reality. She was alone with no family. American soldiers were all over the island. The Japanese could not, would not protect them. She considered her options and she could only think of two: death or survival.

She had no food or supplies, no shelter except this cave filled with a death boat. She would do her best to survive knowing death might find her anyway.

Carefully, she searched the boat for any supplies. Finding none, she crept to the hidden opening of the cave. She was starving, the last meal she could remember was the cold Spam her mother had shared with her… this morning? A day ago?

It was night and the moon had risen full, throwing silver light across the sand. Shigeko wondered if she might risk wandering out and searching for food. Surely the soldiers slept at night like regular people. It was so quiet, she wondered if they might already be gone. She crept out.

The air outside was warm. The beach looked so different from just a few days ago. Where trees had once stood, now splintered trunks shattered in the moon's light. She could see the broken wood, like the bones of the island protruding from sandy flesh. She was hungry enough that she might consider taking candy from a soldier now.

Shigeko crept along the cliff face, headed in the general direction of her home. There might be food left there. They hadn't taken all of it with them when they left. If she searched the outhouse, she might even find more canned meat hidden there. She kept her mind on her hunger. It was all she could handle for now.

Once, she thought she heard voices. She melted into the dark and stayed still. Two women walked by in the road, speaking in low voices. Shigeko wanted to reach out to them but she remembered the woman in the bunker, the panic that had caused her Chiga's death. It was best to avoid other people—any people. People were dangerous.

Her house wasn't far and Shigeko made it there in just over an hour. Travel had been slow. She felt as though the forest was watching her. She wondered if there were soldiers hidden in the shadows or just other hungry scavengers like herself.

She sat hidden within sight of her house for a long time before she dared approach. All sorts of possibilities ran through her mind, none of them good. Maybe soldiers slept inside already—American ones now, not Japanese. What if they had set up booby traps for those who might return? She had heard of trip wires attached to grenade pins.

Finally, she came as near as the outhouse. There was no movement inside, no sounds. The sight of her home was a stab to her chest. The last time she had been here it had been a home instead of a house.

The things that were so ordinary then: Chiga nestled up against her side, overheating her. No matter how many times she shoved him over he would return. The sound of her mother's soft breathing, her father's occasional snort… these things she would never hear again. She pushed the thoughts away.

She came as close as the garden. She knew where to find things to eat, even in the dark. Groping in the wet earth she found sweet potatoes. She wiped them off and ate them raw. She stuffed mouthfuls of greens and fruit into her face, barely taking the time to chew. Still quiet. Shigeko made her way to the well to drink. She studied her quiet house. If she had her mother's woven bags she could carry food back to her hidden cave and stay there until the war left.

Shigeko crept up to the outer walls of her house and peeked inside. Through the partially open door she could see the bedding was still left out. Mother would be upset to know her house was left this way. Shigeko entered her house quietly, like a robber.

She went directly to the small wooden box that kept some of their stores. A paper sack of brown sugar hunks, sweet potatoes, tins of sardines… Shigeko snatched these things out of the box and loaded them into one of her mother's woven bags.

She almost dropped it all when someone moaned behind her in the dark. One of the Japanese soldiers that had stayed with them was laying sideways with his legs crossed as if he had fallen over while sitting. In the dim light from the door Shigeko could see his eyes were open but they were not looking at her. They twitched and rolled back in his head and then forward again. His face was pressed into the wooden floor, blood and drool pooled under his cheek. Why he was there didn't matter. He was there, an unwelcome guest in the first place and now he had come back to die.

Shigeko slid along the wall, sideways. She had meant to bring the bucket back with her, filled with water, but now all her attention was on leaving this house and never returning. She made it to the door as he moaned again. She turned and fled.

Twenty-Six

Yuki, South Okinawa: Freedom of Sorts

"How do you know it's Japanese?" Yuki asked.

Kana pointed. "You can see the Rising Sun painted on the tail."

He gave a whoop and cavorted around the garden. "They are going to blast the Americans away!"

Yuki thought of the soldier giving her father the grenade. She wasn't as happy to see them. The Japanese were not *uchinanchu*, of the island. They were as foreign as the Americans. She wished they would all go away, all the soldiers.

"Let's go watch from the beach!" Kana started running.

Yuki followed the direction he went, but she felt dread at the sky full of soldiers. None of them belonged here. None of her people were part of this war. Her mother had called it *inujini*, a dog's death. A waste of life for no purpose, a terrible payment for loyalty. Dogs only have love, her mother had said. To repay that with death is to lose a part of humanity.

The ocean wasn't far from Kana's house. When Yuki caught up, he was dancing in the sand and surf, kicking both up in sprays around him.

"Run, Americans! The Japanese will chase you cowards out!"

Kana was scaring her. He had a madness. He grabbed up handfuls of sand and threw it at the huge ships that sat on the edge of the horizon like mythical monsters. They were *kaijū,* strange beasts of metal that exhaled toxic fumes.

"Run Americans! Run if you can!"

Kana was screaming like an old woman, cackling and spinning.

The first planes were nearly on the ships now. Yuki waited for them to open fire. They seemed too small for the mammoth ships. How were the tiny soldiers supposed to scare the Americans away with just their bullets?

The planes were flying low, straight at the ships. The Americans were trying to open fire on the agile planes but they were impossible to hit. The closest plane wasn't pulling up but zeroing in on the floating container of men. At the last second, Yuki realized what was happening.

The small plane plummeted into the ship without ever trying to turn away. It was a direct hit, intentional. The impact threw plumes of metal and smoke high into the air where they caught the rays of the setting sun. Sirens screamed across the water, competing with the noise of the plane swarm. Kana stopped running around and just watched, disbelieving, as more planes tried to fly into the American ships. Most of them didn't even make it that close.

The Americans were firing now, giant guns that threw up massive plumes of water. Blots of smoke rose into the sky. Japanese planes were throwing themselves into the water as the ship guns tore through them. They looked like chrysanthemums floating on the sea with petals of fire.

Absently, she wondered if the dolphins could escape the destruction. It wasn't their war. *It's not our war either,* she thought. *So whose war was it?* Her legs lost all their strength and her spirit flowed out through the bottoms of her feet to be lost in the sand. Yuki collapsed to her knees.

Kana was frozen, watching as plane after plane exploded. Some of them connected with the ships, but most plowed into waves. From his tense posture, Yuki thought he might be crying. He too collapsed to his knees, staring ahead at the colossal loss playing out before them.

One of the planes was out of control, wings torn apart from gunfire. It spiraled, wobbling. Yuki saw the wings fold like a bird around the body and then it dove beneath the waves.

Kana was stumbling to his feet. He ran away from her, further down the beach. He was unstable like a drunk. He was screaming at the planes to stop. He hurled driftwood and fistfuls of sand, but this time at the Japanese pilots.

"Why? Why? Why the waste?"

As if in divine answer, a mortar shell from one of the ships flew straight at them. Yuki saw it when it was too late. It froze in the sky for an eternal second while her brain tried to identify the black cylinder hurling through the air. She screamed at Kana as she propelled herself backward. It was aiming right at him.

The world exploded. Sand, sea and shrapnel filled the air before everything went dim. She lay on her back, stunned. The explosions of planes throwing themselves into the ocean were far away. The air was full of dust and smoke. In a rush, she inhaled and then coughed all the breath back out. She stumbled to her feet.

Kana...Kana!

She wasn't sure if she was calling him out loud. Her voice sounded far away. She stumbled toward where Kana had been seconds ago. She thought she might be screaming. Her throat was on fire but there was no sound.

A large part of the beach was gone. There was a crater, like a dish had been set in the sand but it was empty; there was no Kana. She scanned the beach, looking for him.

Ahead of her was a scrap of material. Red velvet with a long tassel of black silk attached. Yuki stumbled toward it. She would unravel this treasure, turn it into something new on her hand loom. She fell to her knees as she picked it up by the silk, trying to shake the sand off. The velvet was so smooth, she couldn't even see the texture of the warp or how the silken threads were attached.

A rapid series of thoughts passed through her brain as fast as machine gun fire. She held the bit of fabric out. It wasn't quite fabric. It was wet, a little red jelly in the silk threads, the lack of weft and thread was more like goat hide when her father butchered…

Her hearing returned in a rush as her own scream exploded from her. She tossed the piece of Kana away from her. As it dropped onto the beach, she saw every grain of sand that stuck to the raw remnant of her only friend.

The explosions and fire blossomed across the sky and sea, a horrid tableau of deadly flora. And then she was running away from it all.

Twenty-Seven

Kaori, North Okinawa: Karmic Carnage

When they were close enough to discern the monotone dialect of the strangers, Hiro stopped. "Here's where I go alone, Kaori. Please don't go away. I don't want to do this alone."

"I won't leave again."

Kaori thought Hiro might be nodding and then he closed his eyes. He didn't move. The men seemed too close. She remembered the soldiers who had her trapped in her own home. Their voices were too close, too loud. Panicked, she tensed to run but she held on. She couldn't lose her brother again now.

Hiro...

Something stirred in her mind. A physical sensation of touch brushed the inside of her skull, making her shiver. He was with her there, her baby brother. She could feel his presence nestling up in her mind. There were no words, only a sense of hushing and heaviness. He was sleeping.

Hiro-shiisaa opened blank dark eyes and looked at Kaori without recognition. In spite of herself, she started. The creature turned slowly with no reaction, no response, and went toward the camp. Unsteady at first, and then it began to move faster until it loped full speed into the clearing ahead.

The soldiers were caught by surprise. A handful of yells competed with each other before ending abruptly. Gunfire erupted and was followed by a chorus of screams. Kaori stayed rooted where she was, terrified, unwilling to witness the carnage unfolding just ahead.

Kaori... don't go too far. I won't find my way back...

Then Hiro went silent again.

Reluctantly, she crept forward in inches. By now the air was filled with the metal tang of gunpowder and blood. Something was on fire ahead. Kaori could see the flames leaping to the sky through the trees. As she moved close enough to have a clear view through the brush, the chaos died down, and the only sounds were a few moans and the flames consuming a square tent. Her brother... *his body*, she reminded herself... was stalking through the camp now, looking for survivors. As he moved, a man tried to crawl away through the sand with his remaining arm. He pitched forward onto his face as the terror moved behind him, raised a massive paw and smashed down. Blood and brain spewed out in jets and the man's skull was flattened.

Kaori collapsed to her knees and vomited. Puke and tears ran down her face. She couldn't catch her breath. Her lungs were constricting from the ragged sobs that shook her. She tried to wipe her chin but she was shaking too badly. A shadow was pulling over her like a blanket blotting out the sun, the sight of a man's thoughts glistening in the sand, her brother's body turning to look at her...

Kaori...

She couldn't do this. She wouldn't answer. She should have left with her mother. This was too much. Too much death. Too much pain. This should have never happened to her. She was going to sleep with Hiro, safe in her mind somewhere.

Kaori... I need your strength. You are my tether.

"Noooo... no..."

Kaori... don't lose me again. I need you.

"I... can't..."

She was going to die. Hiro was going to die. Her parents might be dead already. She imagined her infant sister sinking into the sea, food for fishes. Kaori began sinking herself.

Kaori...

Less insistent, fading, leaving her alone. Kaori's mind began to drift until she thought of Hiro, the last day he was a boy. His brown eyes, always laughing. His small hands, so clever at disrupting her as she tried to work. The sound of his voice as he called out to her, fearful. She had let him go.

Somehow, she was on her knees. She crawled forward, covered in her own sick. She staggered to her feet and looked for Hiro-shiisaa. He was nowhere. She had lost him, but she felt nothing. A numb calm had settled over her. The events outside of her were dull, the gore had lost its bright hues and looked dream-like. The only thing that mattered was they finished this. She would find Hiro.

The camp they had come across was small compared to the number of men she saw camped around her own house. A half dozen bodies spread into two dozen pieces were strewn about. One of the odd, square tents was in flames. The smoke stained the air with a charcoal streak. This would bring more of the men. She spied Hiro standing at the edge of the clearing, waiting for her. More men would be good.

She could hear them crashing through the underbrush. The space their bodies occupied fought with the world around them. They forced their way, trampling a path. Their voices were assaulting. Brash and harsh, a donkey-bray tongue, they crashed and tore their way closer. Kaori waited.

The first ones to clear the woods moved to the side and crouched, guns aimed on her. She was past fear. They saw the carnage and their faces somehow became even paler. One of them shot the ground near her, shouting, but Kaori didn't even flinch. None of this felt real.

Their eyes were on her, the tent engulfed in flame and the dismantled bodies. They were blind to what approached them through the trees until it was too late. The noise they made with their shouting covered Hiro's approach until he skewered one of the men through with his talons.

The men scattered, confused and disoriented. Several of them saw their comrade writhing in the air with stone claws pushed through his chest and sprayed him with bullets in their panic. Two more were caught in this accidental gunfire and fell screaming. Another stood frozen, unable to move.

He held his radio to his mouth but it hung open, useless, until Hiro-shiisaa closed it for him with a blow.

The few that escaped didn't get far as they ran, slowed by the underbrush and sand that caught at their clumsy boots, holding them. Hiro barely loped between the trees as he smashed and crushed all the men he found. Their stink mixed with the smoke and blood.

Kaori followed, gliding through her graphic dream of freedom and vengeance. This story would have a happy ending, but not for everyone. The radio on the ground was still crackling static panic at her until she picked it up. She wasn't sure if the shouting men somewhere else could hear her, and if they could, even understand her words. She spoke anyway, mashing the button on the side as she had seen the soldiers do. The radio went silent.

"Go home."

She dropped the radio. The crackle-static came back but the voices on the other end were silent. Kaori followed her little brother toward the sound of yelling.

Twenty-Eight

Shigeko, Zamami Island: Discovered

Shigeko didn't try to be quiet now. She ran down the middle of the road. The net bag with its cargo of cans banged against her hip, but she couldn't hear it. Her heart was pounding loud enough to alert the whole island to her presence. Wild haired and wild eyed, she fled to the safest place she knew at this time—a hidden suicide boat.

Someone shouted from one of the houses but she only ran faster. There was another shout and then gunfire pelted the road around her. She could feel fragments of stone and dirt kick up onto her legs. She didn't dare stop. Though she was already running as fast as she ever thought possible, somehow she picked up the pace just a little more.

When she reached the beach she dove straight into her little cave, smacking her head against the boat hull hard. With one hand holding her head, she quickly pulled the pampas grass back in place to hide her hollowed out sanctuary. The gunfire and shouting stopped, and she didn't hear anyone following. In spite of this, she didn't dare move a muscle, other than to rub the rising bump on her head.

After some time, she peeked carefully out onto the beach.

It was clear. The only movements were from the occasional crest of white from the waves as they gently lapped the cove beach. There weren't even the sounds of the night birds. From what she could see of the destroyed trees, she wondered if any were still alive. Was anyone she knew alive? The image of the bodies, her Chiga, returned but she forced it back. That was something she couldn't deal with now. Right now she had to survive.

Why she needed to survive was a dangerous question. Perhaps her father had been right. To pull the fork from the grenade would be a fast end, and none of this would matter anymore. She would join her family wherever their spirits had gone—but their bodies would remain rotting in that blown open bunker, bones scattered by animals. She might be the only one left to remember them, what happened to them. The only one who could come back to retrieve their bones to lay in the tomb with the rest of her family. She had to stay alive, if only for that, and staying alive meant she needed to eat.

She dug in the net bag, still hanging around her shoulders. A raw sweet potato was the most delicious thing she had tasted in her life. She opened a can of sardines, the sound of metal peeling open was like a scream in the tiny cave. The smell of the fish in oil was so intense it made her taste buds spasm with hunger. Quietly, she tipped the can up and drank the oil.

She scooped the fish into her mouth with grimy fingers. She wound up eating two tins, inhaling the first, taking time to savor the second. She followed it up with some of the brown sugar rocks from the paper bag. Through the pampas grass, she could see the sun was rising. The island started coming alive with noise. Fewer birds than normal. She carefully put everything away and slipped to the cave mouth to peek outside.

Her world was destroyed. The little cove felt dead. The shrubs and undergrowth were burnt away in patches, the smooth sand scarred from impacts from grenades, or maybe even bigger explosives. At the edge of the water she could see something floating, gently lapping up against the shore with the waves. It looked like a bundle of rags, but the way the crabs were swarming it, Shigeko thought it was something worse.

She backed into her hidden cave, clambered over the little plywood boat and pulled herself and her precious bag of supplies down into the hollow hull. The safest place on the island for her was nestled in a boat designed for death. With this thought playing through her mind on repeat, Shigeko let her mind go numb and drifted into a waking doze.

Shigeko woke up to screaming and gunfire right outside her cave. She could feel the heat of the day seeping in. An even louder explosion hit close enough to make the earth shake and sand from her shallow cave to sprinkle over her. A girl's voice was crying, a woman screamed again and then more gunfire. The woman was silent but the girl was still crying.

More gunfire made Shigeko jump, and then the girl too was quiet.

It is Japanese soldiers on the beach, it has to be, Shigeko thought. *They've come for their boat.*

Of course they had come back for their boat to use against the American attack. She did not think they would be happy to find her there. She scrambled with her bag of supplies to the very back of the shallow cave. Maybe they would pull the boat out without looking in the cave to see her. She did not want any part of their mercy.

The sound of a plane came from overhead followed by louder machine gun fire. She could feel the impact of the bullets pounding into the sand. The Japanese were yelling profanities and firing back. Some of them were screaming in pain rather than rage. Then the plane flew past. There were only a few soldiers left yelling on the beach. The pampas grass was moving—someone was coming into her cave. She saw a soldier's face before she ducked back down.

"It's here!" He turned his head away to shout at the beach.

The sound of the plane returned along with its bigger, louder machine gun fire. A spray of bullets pelted the cave entrance. Shigeko was covered in the sand they sprayed into the air, and the smell of metal smoke choked her. The soldier in the entrance cried out and collapsed. Then the plane was gone again.

There was silence except for the man that now lay half in the cave. He was still alive, his breath coming out in ragged bursts. She imagined his legs laying outside the cave like a beacon, alerting everyone to her hiding spot. She risked a peek over the boat at him.

He was laying twisted, arms outstretched toward the boat as if he was still trying to reach it. The sandy floor around him was soaked in blood. He lay face down, struggling to breathe. Her movement alerted him and he craned his neck up to see her.

"Hey..." he gasped. He spoke Japanese. His breath had a high pitched whistle to it. "Hey..."

From a distance, she could hear the plane returning. The soldier heard it too. He turned to look back at the beach, and then at her. He started trying to crawl forward, into the cave—into her cave. Shigeko shook her head at him.

"No, go away. You can't come in here."

"Help..." He could barely speak. Exhausted, he collapsed. He had lost so much blood, it was running into the cave to pool on depressions in the floor. The plane was nearly there.

"Go out or they will find this place!" Shigeko threw sand at him to discourage him from coming closer. His outstretched hand reached for her, or raised to block the sand she threw, she couldn't tell. The roar of the plane filled the world, and then the machine gun fire came again. It tore through the man and the cave, causing it to partially collapse. Shigeko buried her face in her lap to protect her eyes from the splintered rock and shrapnel. She pressed herself up to the boat for partial shelter. The plane would hit the bombs in the boat. She was going to die anyway.

The plane faded as it went on its way again, but the world was full of screaming that didn't stop until Shigeko realized it was her own. She made herself stop, but she couldn't control the shuddering sobs and shaking.

"Quiet, quiet Shigeko." She had to get control of herself and stay alive. Crying would only let more soldiers know where she was. "Quiet, quiet, quiet..."

She whispered the mantra to herself but it didn't help. She couldn't regulate her breathing. It came out in gasps that shook her body. The more she tried to control it, the worse the racking breath tore her apart. Then she heard the plane returning.

A voice hummed in her ear. It was deep and had a gravel texture to it, like a growl. "*Hūṃ... fiūṃ...fiūṃ...*" It was the song of the female shiisaa, half of the whole. It was enough to make her look up in surprise, but other than the now silent soldier, she was alone. Still, she heard the voice humming.

It was louder and closer than the approaching plane. It eclipsed the sound of explosions elsewhere on the island. It covered her like oil, soaking into her pores, blanketing her in calm. She closed her eyes. Nothing mattered. The plane would shoot the cave and blow it up. It wasn't the end of the world, just her world. She would be with family.

She could barely hear the plane now over the sound of the humming. It was the shiisaa song of the shiisaa—part of the song—but it was enough. She could feel the little clay guardian vibrating in her pocket and she realized the sound was coming from there. She held it to her chest and all worry evaporated. She had her shiisaa. She was still protected.

Then, the plane was gone.

The song faded into silence as well. The sudden quiet made her ears ring.

Twenty-Nine

Yuki, South Okinawa: Dreams and Laughter

Yuki ran blindly, unaware of what landscape she passed through. Her mind was replaying recent scenes from memory, all the things she had refused to think about:

Her father holding the grenade.

Her mother's back as she vanished with Shoji in the dark.

A neighbor named Toshio whose back was ruined with holes full of flies.

A ghost woman walking with her top torn open and smeared in bloody hand prints.

Soldiers that fell from the sky to explode like flaming lilies on the sea.

A scrap of her friend, a bit of velvet and silk, abandoned to crabs.

A bundle of goat meat covered in flies.

She no longer worried about the American soldiers finding her. She was looking for them so she could scream at them like the yokai, and they would end this horror with their guns. She would run at them and claw their faces from their skulls. She shrieked as she ran so they would find her.

Finally, she collapsed. Unable to run farther, she buried her face in the loamy soil of the jungle and screamed into the mud. She gripped the earth, trying to bury herself, willing the soil to open up and swallow her. And then there was a hand on her back, patting her. Someone was telling her to be calm and shushing her gently. She was so surprised, she stopped screaming and looked up.

It was a young woman, not as old as her mother, but she had a daughter clinging to her back. The little girl stared at Yuki with large black eyes, trying to decide if she was going to cry or not. Yuki didn't want to frighten her, so she stopped.

"Good, good. You have to calm down so you don't bring the soldiers here. Come into the cave. We're safe here. I have food for you."

Yuki sat up. The cave? That was where she lost her family. She knew there were many caves on the island, but this one was here now. Her parents might be just inside, safe and wondering who was making all the noise. Yuki nodded, wiped the tears and dirt from her face with her sleeve.

"Yes, please. My family may be inside."

Relieved, the woman helped Yuki to her feet and guided her through a stand of bamboo to the safety of the earth.

The cave was packed with people sitting shoulder to shoulder in the dark. It smelled of feces and sweat. In the earthen dusk, she could barely discern faces. She groped her way through, calling softly for her parents, but no voices answered her. The cave was so tightly packed there was barely room to walk. The voices that did answer her told her to sit down and be quiet so the enemy would not hear. When she was sure her family wasn't there, Yuki made her way back to the entrance. She would leave in the morning and find other caves. She had hope.

Yuki could see a small girl, maybe only about seven. She sat alone so Yuki sat with her. Neither of them said a word but the little girl moved closer, and instinctively Yuki wrapped her arms around her. The little girl shivered violently so Yuki began humming to her to calm her. She could think of no words, nor did she feel she had the spirit to voice them so she softly hummed the song of the shiisaa.

"Afiūṃ...Afiūṃ...Afiūṃ..."

Yuki rocked in rhythm with her humming and the little girl rocked with her. The violent shivering smoothed out and merged with the rocking. Back and forth they swayed, gently. On impulse, Yuki reached into her pocket and pulled out her female shiisaa. She gave it to the girl to hold. The child didn't say a word, but she accepted it. In the last of the light Yuki could see her fist close around the little ball of clay. Yuki continued rocking and humming until eventually she drifted off into sleep...

...and dreamed of her shiisaa as a giant guardian, a protector of them all. She was herself, but she felt expanded, multiplied. Her shiisaa was no longer a round ball of clay with crude features. Now she towered over Yuki, her red clay surface transformed into fragrant fur that shone like burnished copper. Together they traveled the island kingdom, clearing out the invaders. It was a bloody cleansing, but it was essential to restoring the balance.

As she awoke she cried, not wanting to leave this dream. Someone was pulling at her, nudging her awake. As her eyes fluttered open she could still hear her shiisaa whispering to her.

I am with you. Hiro is here.

It was daylight. The woman who had brought her in the night before was nudging her awake, pulling at the little girl still wrapped in her arms. The girl was stiff and her eyes were open, staring blankly at the cave ceiling. Yuki gasped, and let go. She tried to scoot away but there was no room to go far. The woman put her fingers to her lips and started pulling at the little body. Another woman moved forward to help. Together they pulled the little corpse out of the cave, but not before Yuki saw her little dress was caked in blood that blossomed around bullet holes.

She looked around the cave. No one looked at her. Their eyes were turned away to give her privacy. There were no faces she recognized here—no friends or family. The women that removed the little body came back in, gave Yuki a sympathetic look and sat down. After that they kept their eyes down, staring at their knees. There was no reason to stay. The space she occupied was needed. Yuki left.

She didn't know where she was going now. She could hear explosions somewhere on the island. There was gunfire, but she had lost her fear. Last night a little girl died in her arms. Her own parents and Shoji could be gone too. She had watched Kana blow up in front of her eyes. After losing everything, she felt unburdened, lighter. Everything she cared about was gone and she felt calm.

Or maybe I am also just dying, she thought. *Either way, none of it really matters now.*

With nothing left to fear, Yuki noticed how beautiful the morning was. She had lived her entire life here but she had never noticed how the sun gilded all the leaves in gold. Once this land had been a kingdom of its own. This morning, as it was being ripped apart, Yuki could see that magic in everything.

Out of habit she put her hands in her pockets to touch her shiisaa for comfort and found one missing. She remembered. The little girl from last night… she had given it to comfort her. The girl shiisaa was still probably balled up in her little, cold fist. Let her keep it. Yuki imagined soon she might be joining her. She would find her family in this life or the next.

Yuki wandered aimlessly until she reached a beach. She walked out onto the white sandy expanse not caring if she was seen by soldiers. What more could they take away? She knelt and scooped up a handful of sand. If she looked closely she could see the stars among the grains. Her mother used to say they were the stars that fell with the goddess Amamikyo when she set her feet to earth to create this land. Yuki let the sand fall through her fingers, admiring how it flashed in the sun. *This is what life is. We are all falling stars.*

Let the soldiers come with their bullets and bombs.

She was ready.

Thirty

Kaori, North Okinawa: Vengeance

Kaori walked through an island in chaos. Soldiers were running everywhere. They failed to notice the blood covered giant until it was too late. Kaori walked without fear. A single soldier opened fire on her. In her shock induced trance, she didn't notice the bullets whistling past her face. The soldier ceased firing when his head smashed between two massive paws. The rest of his party died nearly as fast and just as oblivious as to who, where or what their enemy was.

The island wasn't big, but at least a quarter of it was covered by the military. Most of the men never knew what hit them. They never determined what was attacking them and the few reports that weren't garbled made no sense. Kaori and Hiro had no trouble finding soldiers. They followed the stink of machine.

In her dream-state, Kaori wondered if there were other guardians protecting the island. They came across unfamiliar scenes of bloodshed, but whether they were traveling in circles or there were other guardians at work didn't matter.

At other times, there was evidence the island itself was doing what it could to expel the invaders. They found the remains of a plane half buried in a sinkhole, twisted metal jutting out of the ground along with a man's legs that had stopped kicking.

A fire broke out elsewhere, rushing down the mountain to flatten a larger camp into ash and charred corpses. The men had been caught unawares by the fire as they tried to figure out what kind of enemy was demolishing their forces. They felt invincible gathered together, but the fire was only able to spread faster as it clung to bubbling flesh. The men became human torches as they ran blindly through the camp. Once the screaming stopped the flames were gone. The fire, having fulfilled its purpose, vanished as quickly as it appeared.

The sea had also shown itself to be unfriendly by washing farther inland than normal. The tide kept rising to flood a depot storing ammunition and supplies. All of it was carried away by the ocean, sealed boxes and canisters bobbing in the receding waves—gifts for other shores.

Time lost meaning in this state. Kaori followed Hiro. He had become little more than a golem in defense of the island. At times he would cease moving and just stand as if he were listening for new directives. When this happened, Kaori would also stand and wait. However long they were in this state, she never felt exhausted. No hunger or thirst… the only thing that mattered was ridding the island of the threat. Her one thought was to stay near her brother no matter who he was or what he did.

Then, without any memory of how she went to sleep, Kaori woke up. They were in the grotto and the sun was just about to rise. How many days had gone by didn't matter. The sky was golden and clean. Once again, garlands of red flowers hung across the water and were draped across the stones. They floated in the still end of the small pool, drifting together to make little floral continents.

For the moment, there were no flat, harsh voices yelling—no toxic stink, no guns firing. It smelled, sounded and felt like home. Kaori sat up to see Hiro sprawled in the tiny pool beside her. He was breathing softly, asleep. Inside, she felt empty. Inside, she felt clean.

"Hiro…"

He opened his eyes and blinked at her.

"What?"

This was her brother again, no matter what body he wore. She was relieved to see the blank look had gone. She was relieved to be herself.

"Do you think they are all gone?"

The past was a nightmare to forget. Flashes of destruction—agonized masks, twisted corpses. That was another life.

"I think so, or I don't think we would be here."

Kaori was hesitant. "We should… go see."

Without a word, Hiro got up and went through the waterfall curtain. Kaori felt reluctant to go into the shadows. She wanted to feel the morning warm on her skin. The tension was gone. The island exhaled and resumed breathing..

Kaori ran down the stone cut path, determined to arrive before her brother. As her feet limp-skipped over the stone she had known all her life, a giddy joy overtook her. By the time she reached the grove she was giggling. She burst from the hidden place and rolled onto the soft grass under the trees. She didn't care if she slipped in rotted fruit.

At about the same moment, Hiro popped up on the lip of the grove. He was with her within seconds. Together, they chased each other as if they were both children again, but the game didn't last as long. In this form Hiro's long legs and reach made the game nearly pointless and Kaori was no longer as quick.

They came from their secret place to see the cost of protecting their home. Bodies were everywhere in different states of destruction. Dismembered limbs hung from vines and jutted out of bushes. Here the air was less fresh. The smell of spoiled meat was carried in the salty breeze.

"I guess we will have to start burying the dead." Kaori dreaded the idea of any more death.

"Let the birds have them." Hiro smacked a partial arm out of a tree.

"Then we'd be just like them, Hiro. If we act like our enemies, we become them."

"You've changed," he said.

"Not as much as you."

The joke hit home and they came onto the beach laughing. The sand was warm and smelled sweet. Kaori ran the tiny star shaped grains between her fingers, watching them fall. Hiro was watching the sea and was the first to see them.

"A boat!"

Kaori couldn't see it yet but she felt dread returning.

"Soldiers? Are there more?"

Hiro squinted against the sun. "No… it's too small." He started trotting toward the sea. "It's a girl! Not soldiers!"

Kaori started running too. Now she could see it, just barely. A bobbing cork on the edge of the ocean's curve, but it was coming in fast with the tide. Hiro was running back and forth in the surf yelling and cavorting.

Then they heard laughter.

Thirty-One

Shigeko, Zamami Island: Boat Trip

S higeko had hours to plan her escape once she decided that was what she needed. She had never left her island, but there was nothing left for her here. A crack split her insides, fragmenting her heart, and she knew, wherever she went, it would not be home. That place no longer existed.

As soon as it was dark, Shigeko took action. The planes had flown overhead all day, and with the sound of every single one, she waited for a torrent of gun fire to rain down on her again, detonating the bombs that shared her cave.

The dead soldier was another matter. He had died reaching out to her for help. His eyes were still open, staring at her the rest of the day. If she thought that was horrible, it got worse as the cave grew dark. She was certain he was still alive, moving toward her. She could hear the sand moving beneath his body.

She wondered if she had also died. All day long she'd been talking to her remaining shiisaa. She'd babbled about the soldier coming back to life and the bomb would exploding to end her bid for survival. Her shiisaa answered her and told her how she could survive. It was this plan Shigeko followed now.

At one point she had dozed and dreamed her shiisaa had become a giant beast covered in short, red golden fur that wandered the island with her, but also not with her, and they drove the invaders back. Together they protected their home. In the dream she called her Hiro.

Hiro, her shiisaa, sang to her frequently during that long day. It soothed her as it had always done. Even a partial song was better than none, and in a fractured world, it was enough. She had stared into the dead soldier's eyes for hours, held together by the rhythmic *Hūṃ...hūṃ...hūṃ...* Until now.

Once she felt she would be hidden by the dark, she summoned all her grit and slithered out the mouth of the shallow cave to slide past the corpse. She imagined his stiff fingers suddenly becoming animated to snatch at her as she scrambled past. Outside, she turned back to face him, ready to spring if he came after. Fully dead, he didn't move.

Her next step was to remove his body. His feet were much less frightening than his dead eyes. Shigeko grabbed hold of his boots and pulled him free. He wasn't as heavy as she expected, but his stiffened corpse didn't slide out of the cave well. His body snagged against the rubble and rocks that had fallen, but Shigeko was energized by fear. His body was in the way of her escape. His body must go.

Finally she had the corpse removed and rolled to one side. He was starting to smell and she was grateful she had listened to her mythical Hiro. Once she had the body removed, she went to work on the rubble from the cave's partial collapse. Moving with purpose, she tossed the stones she could pick up and rolled away the stones she couldn't.

Once the pathway from the cave was clear, Shigeko piled her bag of supplies in the boat and pushed it out. Her fear gave her strength and she moved by herself what had taken three soldiers to move before. She wondered if she had always been capable of more than she imagined.

Getting the boat up the incline was difficult, but once she had it up on the flatter beach she found it easier to pull. She tried not to look at the dead soldier as she passed. The crabs had found him. Just past him lay the body of a woman and a child. Shigeko remembered the screams earlier. *In the end we are all the same,* she thought. *We can only be our own enemies. We can only protect ourselves from ourselves.*

She pulled the boat along the beach and up to the water's edge. There she climbed aboard and opened the hatch to the bomb with the intention of removing it. She had expected it to be like a grenade but it was so large and heavy she worried it might explode as she rolled it off. Too scared to touch it, the bomb stayed.

Shigeko took a minute to look at her home island. She may never see it again. She searched for something she recognized and found little in the shredded treeline. The beach was pitted with craters and bodies swarming with scavengers. What was the point of it all? What was the fighting over, and why was her island in the middle of it?

There was nothing to miss. This was no longer her home. Shigeko pulled the boat into the water until she was waist deep, and it started floating on its own. She climbed up. Silently she paddled with her hands, away from the shore and toward the open sea.

Once she made it to the deeper water she let the current pull her outwards until the shore seemed far enough away. Only then did she feel it was safe to start the engine of the boat. The engine noise was loud enough to wake the whole island. Heart pounding, she steered it out toward the black horizon with no direction except whispers from a voice in her head.

As Shigeko slipped away from her home, she felt a part of herself collapse. Like a shelf of sand, it crumbled and was absorbed by the galaxy of ocean she now sped across. Fear, anger and pain disintegrated into the ocean wind to fall behind her. The moon overhead was bright. Her world would never be the same, but in the silvery shimmer of freedom none of that mattered. Darkness would come, and light would return.

She let her mind drift off into daydreams of a grotto draped in flower garlands and hidden groves. Her dream shiisaa Hiro sang to her—*Hūṃ... fiūṃ...fiūṃ...*and she let her hands go slack on the wheel. She had no idea what direction to go, so it didn't matter where she went. As long as she traveled forward she would end up somewhere. It was with these thoughts that Shigeko drifted through the dark. At some point the little boat ran out of gas. She had no fear as she listened to the engine sputter and die. She knew her Hiro was with her and nothing else mattered.

Thirty-Two

It All Comes Together

Shigeko dreamed of laughter.

It was the Hiro in her dream. They were on a sandy beach with stars falling from the sky. Dawn had risen, a rosy gold sheen burning into the blue. All the pain in the world had fragmented her into three pieces. She was only a shard of herself but she had never felt more whole, more alive. She was a trio of herself and with herselves was Hiro.

Fur the color of the dawn, his…her…*their* mane was a mass of copper curls. The fearsome rage of a lion and the loyalty of a dog combined into this magnificent giant that was rolling through the star sand laughing like a little boy.

Shigeko jerked awake.

The sun had actually risen finally. The sky was on fire in a celestial panorama that caused her to tear up, grateful for a dawn she hadn't been promised. It was a gift. The tide was bringing her into a beach. She was not yet dead. Never had Shigeko seen anything as lovely as that sunrise. She was not dead yet, not this moment and maybe not even today.

The wind passed over the island, bringing the sound of laughter to her. She squinted her eyes against the sun. Maybe she was still dreaming. As she drifted closer with the tide, she thought she could see someone sitting in the sand. Perhaps a girl her age. It was hard to tell.

Then something flashed further down the beach and caught her eye. It was red, flashing like red fire as it ran. Like a massive horse… some kind of beast….

Before she had time to wonder if she was dead, insane, or both, Shigeko was screaming into the wind, screaming and jumping up and down.

"Hiro! Hiro! Hiro!"

***

Someone was yelling. Yuki heard a voice screaming from far off. In the water, there was a tiny boat coming in fast with the tide. On it was what looked like a girl jumping up and down like she was demented. It sounded like the girl was yelling the name Hiro.

And then she saw him…her…*them* running down the beach toward her, shaking a massive mane of fire and gold, with all the magnificence of a dragon and the fierce love of a phoenix rolled up into the body of a giant puppy. Behind him hobbled a girl about her own age, laughing and kicking sand in spite of her limp. Yuki stood up, stunned and hopeful, and ran toward them shouting.

"Hiro! Hiro! Hiro!"

***

Kaori couldn't keep up to Hiro but it didn't matter. He looked like a giant Tora Inu pup made of copper and gold. It was hard not to be overcome by the silliness of his playful demeanor. There was someone on the beach ahead of them yelling and running. To her left she could see the girl on the boat had jumped into the water and was swimming to shore fast.

"Hiro! Hiro, slow down!" But Hiro-shiisaa was not listening. He was springing toward the girl on the beach as fast as he could. From the corner of her eye she could see the girl from the boat was stumbling out of the surf. Both girls were running straight at her yelling. Kaori was hearing things. It sounded like they were all yelling the same thing.

"Hiro! Hiro! Hiro!"

Thirty-Three

Regaining Balance

The three girls collided on the beach. In the middle of them was the giant, cavorting shiisaa. They danced, springing and twisting in the air, unbelievably bright. Like rose tinted gold, like copper flame they spun in the air, their flashing mane blinding the girls. When they landed, all three girls collapsed onto them, breathing in the scent of salt, blossoms and amber spice. The girls embraced them, sinking into the sweet warmth of that red fur and then collapsed onto each other. They tumbled to the sand in a heap.

The dazzling golden red blinked out. Dawn was well past and three girls sat in the sand stunned. A red clay shiisaa towered behind them, weathered surface pocked from years of salt spray. Its eyes scanned the horizon, looking for dragons. Kaori's confusion turned to panic when she saw the shiisaa.

"No! Hiro! You can't leave me now!"

She ran her hands over the clay figure seeking any sign of warmth or life. She had found her brother; to lose him again so soon broke her spirits. She wept, face pressed against the rough clay, hoping for a whiff of Sagari-bana. She smelled nothing but earth.

Yuki went to her and cautiously put her arm around Kaori.

"Did you know Hiro?"

Kaori turned to her, wiping tears onto her sleeve.

"Did *you* know Hiro?"

Yuki nodded.

"Hiro is the shiisaa my baaban made for me." Shigeko had remained where she was in the sand, watching the other two. Yuki let go of Kaori and they both sat down, cross legged. The guardian statue sat between them, casting a shadow forward on the sand.

"Hiro is my brother."

Now Yuki looked confused.

"Your brother... is a shiisaa."

Kaori opened her mouth to answer, but the words froze in her throat. Her eyes were staring out to see a flat watercraft with a handful of soldiers coming to shore. She jumped to her feet and they all turned to see.

Yuki thought of a soldier training a gun barrel on her as a dead mother watched and got to her feet. Shigeko remembered a soldier leering at her in a classroom, frightening Ms. Toma and insinuating worse. She stood up as well. None of them spoke as the soldiers ran the boat up on the beach and started jumping out.

The three had an unspoken sisterhood, bonded by trauma. None was willing to break the trinity they had formed. They stood together, hearts racing, watching the soldiers pull the boat up to shore. The shiisaa that somehow belonged to each of them stood at their backs. One of the soldiers ran ahead with his gun out, scanning the treeline. When he saw the three girls standing by the statue, he shouted and waved for them to approach.

None of them moved.

The soldier lowered his gun at them. Other soldiers were lowering their rifles, aiming in their direction. They yelled words none of the girls could understand. He thrust his gun at them to make a point.

"I'm not going to him," whispered Shigeko. She was thinking of the five women in the long house that had to keep an army of men satisfied. "He can shoot me."

Most of the soldiers had hopped off their craft and were busy pulling in the little boat Shigeko had arrived on.

Yuki stepped back. "Maybe we can hide behind Hiro. Maybe he will protect us." She was remembering a yokai in a torn kimono with blood smeared across her breasts and a shattered face.

The men were arguing with each other now, gesturing at the girls who were all taking small, imperceptible steps back.

"Not all soldiers are bad but we have to fend for ourselves," said Kaori. Her thoughts were with a soldier, a big brother, that was trapped by this war as much as her. Her hand slid over the bag slung across her back and she felt the stiff paper of the photo he had given her.

The soldiers had come to a consensus and were coming up the beach toward them.

The girls stood still on the beach, frozen with indecision. There was no place to run to, nowhere was safe. At least on this patch of sand they had each other. At least here they had Hiro, clay statue or not. It was more than any of them had alone.

"Hiro has always helped me, even when I was too scared to recognize him. He will help us now." Kaori was surprised at how little fear she felt—at how little she felt at all. "Let them come."

To calm herself, she started humming the song of the shiisaa. It was low, just for her and her new sisters. It did calm her, the hum grew stronger, deeper. It seemed to rise from the sand and vibrate the air at their backs. Shigeko and Yuki, both well familiar with this sound, joined in.

You can see in the dark...

The voice echoed through their thoughts, cooling and sweet like starlight. It smoothed the fear trembling inside their ribs and dampened the panic. It was like the fresh breath of a storm, the return of calm after chaos.

They all knew this voice. They each heard it plenty when they were young enough to speak with shiisaa.

You are remembering to hear...

The voice was deeper and golden like brass. Warm like morning after a cold night. It enveloped them, shielded them in an invisible barrier of fierce love. Around them, the noon air shimmered with heat. It was two voices, a binary, blending with their own.

"*Afiūṃ…Afiūṃ…Afiūṃ…*"

The soldiers stopped advancing. Behind the three women stood a lion dog statue that looked wrong—the dull clay shone like copper when they blinked. The shadow of the sun sat on the face just enough to give the appearance of black eyes that were like twin orbs full of stars. The mane shimmered in the heat giving the appearance of thick and flaming fur. Though night was long past, the cool scent of Sagari-bana wafted among them with the spicy odor of turmeric and salt.

"*Afiūṃ…Afiūṃ…Afiūṃ…*"

The women sang louder, their voices gathering together as one as they hummed the song of their youth, remembered from dreams. It sang in their blood, etched itself in the air before them, reordered the stars in the sand. The shells on the beach began to vibrate around the men, spinning away. The water receded, beaching the two boats. Fear spread among the soldiers like something contagious.

The first soldier knelt down and lowered his rifle at the trio. Eyes closed, overcome by their spirits, none of the three women noticed. His finger pressed the trigger, the sights trained on Kaori's head… and then the world shattered.

The girls were all blown back by the sudden force and knocked off their feet. A shock wave blew over them, flattening the sparse beach grasses at the tree line. The ordinary day splintered into screams. The brilliant white sand was stained with blood and men.

Shigeko sat up to see the beach littered with flesh instead of men. Before long, silence settled over the tableau of shattered boats.

"I stole that boat from soldiers," said Shigeko. "It carried a bomb."

"That was for Kana." Yuki had sat up now too. The beach looked too familiar. She expected planes to fly overhead on a mission to be no more than blossoms of fire on the sea. She tried to remember the broken face of the yokai, Toshio's lost shoe… the last time she saw her mother. The color in those memories had faded, the emotions bled together and muted. Her heart was broken, but it still pumped.

Shigeko too felt a vacuum had formed around the hurt that had lodged in her chest. It insulated the pain, lessened the loss. She had lost everything, but she was no longer alone. Together, they were a sisterhood. They were a new family formed from broken parts. Like Kintsugi, mending something shattered with gold, they were stronger now.

"We won't be hurt again," said Kaori. "But neither will we hurt."

They joined hands and walked together away from the beach. The way ahead was uncertain. The way behind was stained in blood. The moment they had was perfect because it was the only promise they had. Together, they made the most of it.

It was all they could do. It was enough.

Afterword

Inujini is my first novel. While I've written plenty of shorter books, this story was my own personal coming-of-age story along with my three protagonists Kaori, Shigeko and Yuki. It was a book I never thought I would write, but shortly after finishing *Tortured Willows* I realized I wanted to tell a story from my own history—not from an Asian perspective but a Ryukyuan specific perspective.

Ryukyuans aren't Japanese. They are an indigenous people similar to the Native Americans in the United States. Like the Native Americans, they have had their land taken from them. Also like the Native Americans, few people listen to their requests to have their homes returned.

I'm only 25% Ryukyuan. It's just enough to allow me to tell this story, my fictional version of the Battle of Okinawa. The rest of me is Caucasian enough to feel like I have a voice. I have never wanted to use it until I learned what it meant to be Ryukyuan.

These are people of deep magic. From the beginning when Amamikyo first set foot to the sea to create the first lands and people, the Ryukyuan have passed that tradition on through their priestesses. The verbal tradition has maintained that holiness, a sacredness in every day. There is no written form of the Ryukyuan language. It is a tongue of spirit that lives in memory.

The utaki, or holy places, are much the same as since the beginning of recorded history. Sacred groves—a union of earth, air, fire and water— the Ryukyuans have always lived in harmony with their environment. Recognizing that women and men are different but equal, there is no history of suffragettes, or need for it. Equality, love and stewardship come naturally to these people who view spirit as essential as body. Non-divisionary, they have buried all the dead from a battle not their own with equal reverence. As a result, they are known for being the longest lived people on the earth, and some of the happiest, in spite of the prejudice, oppression, suppression and bias they have been subject to. These people could teach the world some valuable lessons. Instead, their culture and history is being systematically wiped away by governments that are only interested in keeping a strategic location.

Much of what I wrote in this story is true. The Japanese did keep five Korean prostitutes on hand to service an island of 1,000 soldiers. The soldiers did call the locals *dojin*, or aboriginals. The Ryukyuans were told they were lucky it was not their own daughters and wives. Many Ryukyuans died in compulsory mass suicides. Afterwards, the survivors were often tried as war criminals and imprisoned for the murder of their loved ones despite the fact it was done under Japanese order. If you want to know more about the real stories that inspired the pieces of this one, please find them listed in the next section.

Also true in this story is Shigeko's claim that the Ryukyuan Kingdom (now called Okinawa Prefecture) was considered one of the most hospitable people in the world. The Himeyuri Gakutotai, the Lily Princesses Student Corps is another sad reality that resulted in the loss of 211 high school girls and 16 teachers when they were enlisted as medical help and then abandoned.

I called this story *Inujini* because it means a dog's death—a poor reward for a loyal and loving friend. Another name might have been Kintsugi, the art of repairing broken treasures with gold and other precious metals. Behind this art is a mindset that considers breakage and repair as part of an object's history, rather than something to hide.

This is what I hope for this book. As a result of what has been done, the Ryukyuans are a fragmented people. The languages are on UNESCO's endangered languages list. Much of the history and cultural practices have been forbidden. Many Ryukyuans claimed to be Japanese in hopes their children could escape the bias. As a result, much has been lost—families, history, identity.

This book is my way to try for Kintsugi of my family. I hope this story and others like it can help to knit our history back together and raise enough awareness to return the Ryukyuan Kingdom back to her people. This is our history, but we can mend it. Our stories and art are the precious metals that create something new from our shards—something even better.

This story is focused on Okinawa, a place significant to me, but the story is universal. There is no enemy to point the finger at. We can't wholly blame cultural privilege, imperialism, gender… sadly it's human nature to oppress and dominate regardless of who we are. We do it on a small, everyday scale and we do it globally. As soon as we recognize this, we can stop pointing fingers and get busy evolving.

There are no more excuses to act like cave dwellers. That is our responsibility as individuals to be better, to resist petty anger and to operate on an elevated plane. We can choose kindness and love to create our beautiful existence in our own image.

We can be the gold that mends a broken world.

Angela Yuriko Smith
Rio do Sul, Santa Catarina, Brasil
8 December 2023

Shiisaa: The Guardians of Okinawa

In the vibrant cultural tapestry of current day Okinawa, few symbols are as iconic and deeply ingrained as the Shiisaa, or Shisa. These lion-dog figures, perched on rooftops or guarding entrances, are not just decorative elements but they are also the embodiment of a rich tradition that blends mythology, spirituality, and art. But where do shiisaa come from? What do they symbolize? Finally, what is their place in Okinawan-Ryukyuan society today?

Origins of Shiisaa

The Shiisaa's roots can be traced back to the Ryukyuan Kingdom, an independent nation that consisted of the Ryukyu Arc, a chain of volcanic and coral islands that stretch southwest from Kyushu to Taiwan. Shiisaa are believed to have originated from the Chinese guardian lions, introduced to Okinawa through the kingdom's trade and cultural exchanges with China and other Asian countries.

Just like Shigeko tells Chiga in my story, there is a popular legend that narrates the story of the shiisaa's origin. As per the story, a village on the islands was terrorized by a sea dragon. The Ryukyuan king, gifted with a lion-dog figurine by a Chinese emissary, used it to scare away the dragon. This event led to the creation of lion-dog statues, believed to protect against evil spirits. The shiisaa thus emerged as a guardian figure, blending the features of a lion and a dog, reflecting both Chinese influence and indigenous

Okinawan-Ryukyuan beliefs.

Another legend revolves around what is commonly thought of as the oldest surviving shiissaa statue on the islands. In the village of Tomimori, near Kochinda town, the village was plagued by recurring fires, which caused constant distress and loss of property among its inhabitants. Seeking a solution, the villagers turned to Saiozui, a Feng Shui master, for his wisdom and guidance.

Saiozui's interpretation attributed the frequent fires to the influence of Mt. Yaese, a nearby mountain. In Feng Shui, the natural landscape plays a crucial role in influencing the energy, or chi, of a place. Saiozui's analysis possibly indicated that Mt. Yaese was a source of strong, perhaps unbalanced, yang energy that manifested in the form of fires.

His recommendation was to erect a stone shiisaa statue facing the mountain because shiisaa are regarded as powerful guardians that ward off evil spirits and bring good fortune. By placing a shiisaa statue to face Mt. Yaese, the villagers were not just following a Feng Shui remedy; they were invoking the protective powers of these mythic creatures to shield their village from harm.

The legend concludes that since the installation of the shiisaa, the village of Tomimori has been spared from fires, a testament to the statue's protective efficacy. This story is a beautiful illustration of the shiisaa's significance in Okinawan-Ryukyuan culture. It reflects the deep respect and reverence for nature, the belief in the power of guardians and symbols, and the reliance on traditional wisdom to solve contemporary problems.

This legend, like many others associated with shiisaa, underscores their role beyond mere ornamentation. They are seen as integral to the spiritual and physical well being of a community, embodying a cultural heritage that seamlessly blends folklore, spirituality, and a harmonious coexistence with the natural world.

Symbolic Meaning of Shiisaa

Shiisaa are typically seen in pairs, with one having an open mouth and the other a closed mouth. The open-mouthed shiisaa, the male, is said to ward off evil spirits, while the closed-mouthed one, the female, keeps good spirits in. This duality symbolizes the balance between yin and yang, an essential concept in traditional Chinese and Okinawan-Ryukyuan philosophy. The shiisaa's fierce and vigilant expressions embody strength and protection, often seen as guardians of well-being.

Beyond their protective role, shiisaa are also symbols of Okinawan-Ryukyuan identity. They reflect the islands' unique cultural heritage, a blend of indigenous traditions and external influences. This syncretism is a testament to the island's history as a hub of maritime trade, where diverse cultural elements harmoniously coalesced.

Shiisaa in Architecture

Traditionally, shiisaa are placed on rooftops or at the gates of homes, temples, and businesses. Their role in architecture is both functional and aesthetic. They serve as talismans, believed to protect buildings and their inhabitants from misfortune. Aesthetically, they add a distinctive character to islander architecture, often crafted with artistic flair and creativity.

The design of shiisaa varies widely, from simple and stylized to intricate and realistic. Some are made of ceramic, while others are carved from stone or wood. The variety in their design reflects the individuality of the artisans and the evolving artistic trends.

Contemporary Uses and Cultural Significance

In contemporary times, the role of shiisaa has expanded beyond their traditional use. They have become emblematic of Okinawa-Ryukyuan culture, appearing in various forms of art, souvenirs, and even in popular culture. Shiisaa motifs are found in textiles, ceramics, and jewelry, making them a popular item for both locals and tourists.

Shiisaa also play a role in modern cultural events and festivals in Okinawa. They are featured in parades, dances, and other cultural performances, symbolizing the islands' spirit and heritage. The shiisaa dance, in particular, is a popular performance in Okinawan festivals, where performers wearing shiisaa costumes enact scenes of driving away evil spirits and bringing good fortune.

Moreover, the shiisaa has become a symbol of resilience and identity for Okinawans, especially in the context of the islands' complex history, including their experience during World War II and subsequent American administration. The shiisaa stands as a steadfast reminder of the islander's enduring spirit and cultural richness.

The shiisaa of Okinawa are more than mere statues; they are a vivid representation of the islands' history, culture, and beliefs. From their mythical origins to their contemporary manifestations, they continue to be a significant cultural symbol in Okinawa. They epitomize the blend of indigenous and foreign influences that shape Okinawan-Ryukyuan identity, serving as guardians not just of physical spaces but of the islands' rich heritage. In a rapidly changing world, the enduring presence of shiisaa stands as a testament to the resilience and uniqueness of Okinawan-Ryukyuan culture.

Uchinaaguuchi Phrases

There are also many languages spoken, including Uchināguchi, spoken primarily in the southern half of the island of Okinawa. Central Okinawan distinguishes itself from the speech of Northern Okinawa, which is classified independently as the Kunigami language. UNESCO designated the languages of Amami, Kunzan (Kunigami), Uchinaa (Okinawa), Myaaku (Miyako), Yaima (Yaeyama), and Dunan (Yonaguni) as endangered.

Here are some common phrases:

Hello (male) · Haisai
はいさい

Hello (female) · Haitai
はいたい

Thank you. · Nifee Deebiru
にふぇーでーびる

Nice to meet you. · Hajimiti yaasai
はじみてぃ　やーさい

What's your name? · U-namee ya nuu yaibiiga?
うなめーや　ぬー　やいびーが

How are you? · Ganjuu yaibiimi?
がんじゅー　やいびーみ

Sources:

10 Okinawan (Uchinaaguchi) phrases to learn before your next trip to Okinawa https://www.kanasa.co.uk/okinawan-essential-words-phrases-uchinaaguchi/

Books About Ryukyuan Culture

1. *Stars in the Sand: An Okinawan Shimanchu Legend for Kids* by Kyra Starr
2. *Estrelas na Areia: uma lenda Shimanchu de Okinawa para crianças* by Kyra Starr, Translated by Luiz Peters
3. *Ezra's Ghosts: Stories* by Darcy Tamayose
4. *Speak, Okinawa: A Memoir* by Elizabeth Miki Brina
5. *Tortured Willows: Bent. Bowed. Unbroken.* by Angela Yuriko Smith, Geneve Flynn, Christina Sng, Lee Murray
6. *Night in the American Village: Women in the Shadow of the U.S. Military Bases in Okinawa* by Akemi Johnson
7. *The Girl with the White Flag* by Tomiko Higa and Dorothy Britton
8. *Chiburu: Anthology of Hawaii Okinawan Literature* edited by Lee A. Tonouchi
9. *Okinawan Princess: Da Legend of Hajichi Tattoos* by Lee A. Tonouchi
10. *Oriental Faddah and Son* by Lee A. Tonouchi
11. *Women of the Sacred Groves: Divine Priestesses of Okinawa* by Susan Sered
12. *Ancient Ryukyu: An Archaeological Study of Island Communities* by Richard Pearson
13. *The Last Sakura: Tales of The Yuta* by Ashley Nakanishi
14. *The Ryukyu Kingdom: Cornerstone of East Asia* by Mamoru Akamine
15. *Visions of Ryukyu: Identity and Ideology in Early-Modern Thought and Politics* by Gregory Smits
16. *Tattooing in Okinawa* by Eric Shahan et al

17. *Tattooing in Okinawa Vol. 2* by Eric Shahan and Obara Kazuo
18. *Folktales Of Okinawa* by Shoji Endo
19. *GIFT OF A BLUE BALL: Path of a Fortune-teller in Okinawa* by Jeff Tuthill
20. *Okinawa: A People and Their Gods* by Robinson
21. *Okinawa: The History of an Island People* by George H. Kerr
22. *Okinawa Kwaidan, True Japanese Ghost Stories and Hauntings* by Ron Dutcher
23. *The Ghosts of Okinawa* by Jayne Hitchcock

Further Reading

Battle of Okinawa Timeline
 https://www.preceden.com/timelines/317234-battle-of-okinawa

Buusaa
 https://www.facebook.com/Loochoonukwa/photos/101596924588559
79

Typhoon of Steel: Survivors faced hardships in US camps, returning home
 https://mainichi.jp/english/articles/20210707/p2a/00m/0na/010000c

Ex-Okinawa Governor Masahide Ota, who battled U.S. bases, dies at 92
 https://www.reuters.com/article/us-japan-okinawa-ota/ex-okinawa-g
overnor-masahide-ota-who-battled-u-s-bases-dies-at-92-idUSKBN1930
VX

Moon Goddess and Shrine Maidens: Women in Ancient Ryūkyūan Warfare
 https://ryukyu-bugei.com/?p=7730

The Kitchen God of Sefa Utaki
 https://en.japantravel.com/okinawa/the-kitchen-god-of-sefa-utaki/555
86

No pockets? No problem. See how Japanese men carried personal items on

their kimonos.
https://www.washingtonpost.com/lifestyle/style/no-pockets-no-proble m-see-how-japanese-men-carried-personal-items-on-their-kimonos/201 7/03/10/666506ca-0296-11e7-b9fa-ed727b644a0b_story.html

Kijoka banana fiber cloth
https://kogeijapan.com/locale/en_US/kijokanobashofu/

Okinawa Japanese Kamikaze Attack on US Navy Fleet WW2 Footage April 1945
https://www.youtube.com/watch?v=ZpSuE9BYuj4

Intense Footage of Kamikaze Attacks During WWII
https://www.youtube.com/watch?v=PsI79eO23K0

19 Hours in Kamikaze Hell
https://warfarehistorynetwork.com/article/19-hours-in-kamikaze-hell /

Himeyuri students (Princess Lily)
https://en.wikipedia.org/wiki/Himeyuri_students

Itoman, Okinawa (Himeyuri Butai)
https://en.wikipedia.org/wiki/Itoman,_Okinawa

Turmeric Tea
http://blog.seasonwithspice.com/2011/11/okinawa-turmeric-tea-healt h-benefits.html

Brown Sugar from Okinawa
https://artofeating.com/brown-sugar-from-okinawa/

Okinawan Ritual of Washing the Bones of Deceased Family Members https://www.tokyoweekender.com/2018/06/a-new-film-by-gori-explores-the-okinawan-ritual-of-washing-the-bones-of-deceased-family-members/

The Language of "Racial Mixture": How Ainoko became Haafu, and the Haafu-gao Makeup Fad
https://www.usfca.edu/center-asia-pacific/perspectives/v14n2/okamura

Okinawan Women's Stories of Migration: From War Brides to Issei
https://books.google.com/books?id=yixcEAAAQBAJ&pg=PT97&lpg=PT97&dq=where+did+okinawan+burn+their+bodies+for+burial&source=bl&ots=gnHtz2U1ab&sig=ACfU3U0dyI5vQn_XBhayIaJmc3IqI0GgFQ&hl=en&sa=X&ved=2ahUKEwjAuLDDmfj4AhV5g4kEHY_zBscQ6AF6BAg4EAM#v=onepage&q=where%20did%20okinawan%20burn%20their%20bodies%20for%20burial&f=false

Police officer dispatched from Osaka insults protesters in Okinawa
https://www.japantimes.co.jp/news/2016/10/19/national/police-officer-dispatched-osaka-insults-protesters-okinawa/

About the Invasion of the Kerama Islands by U.S. Forces
https://zamami-peace.net/en/map/

Type 97 grenade
https://en.wikipedia.org/wiki/Type_97_grenade

Suicide Boats
https://www.youtube.com/watch?v=PftlQxGve_M

The Shinyo Kamikaze Boat - Japan's World War 2 Desperation
https://www.youtube.com/watch?v=Zjxk6z5YK2U

Bunkers

https://www.google.com/search?q=Kokumin+School+bunker+ww2&rlz=1C1VIQF_enUS976US976&sxsrf=ALiCzsaW5LCPXbPm3Yqw8rApe5L2tT6t-w:1658916987907&tbm=isch&source=iu&ictx=1&vet=1&fir=_dp4M4QzcZpxQM%252C6K3YJEgKcMwJTM%252C_%253BlZK7uCHAqcanLM%252CNIEo849okBMCCM%252C_%253BO1j88_cvoh6TmM%252CNIEo849okBMCCM%252C_%253B502NuWrrXzteJM%252CeiEC5hQ-RbYoTM%252C_%253Bt6RYr43YZPcHJM%252CL594FbuLDkzjTM%252C_%253BkGmLSqc9HyyiMM%252CQ0Pym1sJLSvG-M%252C_%253Bebw04bLCh5x5AM%252Cth_yp1qWWeFGzM%252C_%253BO4onniFJ_lzCAM%252CNIEo849okBMCCM%252C_%253B9es9PMszSiJIxM%252CzEqsxTVgzxab-M%252C_%253BDIgGEZBPwlpZjM%252CX6J5cW9qE0Vb_M%252C_&usg=AI4_-kRB2l8ZYoV4HNIEnn5Ud87lunvOcQ&sa=X&ved=2ahUKEwjGo5qu65j5AhUpATQIHVu9B7kQ9QF6BAgkEAE#imgrc=O1j88_cvoh6TmM

Okinawa: The Costs of Victory in the Last Battle

https://www.nationalww2museum.org/war/articles/okinawa-costs-victory-last-battle#:~:text=Some%20110%2C000%20Japanese%20and%20conscripted,population%20died%20during%20the%20battle

Thank you, first of all, for reading. Every page turned, every comment, share, message and tear is a priceless gift. Without you, the reader, there is no point in me writing anything more than a grocery list.

Special thanks also to my husband Ryan Aussie Smith who works hard to keep the bills paid so I can follow a passion.

Thank you to my daughter Kyra Starr for her unquestioning support delivered in the form of countless book covers, graphics, and advice. I'm sure she has taught me much more than I have her in our shared lifetimes. She also had the good sense to marry Luiz Peters, conveniently, a translator in quite a few languages.

Thank you to my daughter Emily, a linguist who has humored my many questions about the Japanese and Ryukyuan languages. I often think she inherited my multi-lingual Uncle Shigaru's ability to think in so many languages. Probably because she used to call him "Uncle Sugar," which I think he must have loved.

Thanks to my oldest son Dakota who once advised me that it was okay to be "a stoic." As I remember it, I then had to ask my teenage son what a stoic was and then marvel at his deep wisdom. A few times in my life people have accused me of being smart. I think they must be confusing me for my kids.

Much gratitude also to my son Aaron who has had to fend for himself when it came to mealtime and became a pretty good cook along the way. He has graciously made his own dinner many times while I was off in some closet writing. He has usually been kind enough to make dinner for the rest of us as well. He is also the person who did the lay out work for this book.

Thank you to my mother who helped the story come to life by filling me in on all the family history she can remember. My writing path through the Unquiet books has been my way to understand our relationship better. Much love to both my parents.

Much love also to my writer family and friends, particularly Alma Katsu for both friendship and foreword, Lee Murray and Maxwell I. Gold for actually being there in the horrible month when I wrote this, and all the Unquiet Sisters who have become an force to be reckoned with. Thank you to the Ryukyuan friends I've met along this journey, including the Okinawa Association of America, Inc. (OAA) (oaamensore.org/).

Finally, to my Ryukyuan family: great-grandmother Kana Kobashigawa, great-grandfather Kana Kayoda, my grandmother Yuriko Kayoda, my uncle Shigaru Kayoda and the rest of my ancestors and family whose names I know, and whose names I don't know… I hope I have not taken too many liberties with this story. Forgive me for what I've told wrong. I tried to pluck your words for the future without bruising the past.

Did you enjoy this book?

Word-of-mouth recommendations and online reviews are critical to the success of any book. If you enjoyed this book, please tell your friends about it and consider leaving a review at your favorite book seller or library's website.

For Authors: Authortunities

Authortunities is a weekly calendar newsletter designed specifically for writers to find all the author opportunities they need in a single, curated format. Open submission calls, contests, workshops, open mics, grants and more, in your inbox every Saturday.

Organized by emoji, *Authortunities* contains four weeks of valuable opportunities for authors. Enjoy the next two weeks of opportunities at no cost. Access the entire four weeks of opportunities for just $5.55 a month.

However you take advantage of it, your *Authortunities* are waiting for you.

https://authortunities.substack.com/freemonth
Exercise your writes. Get published. Make change.

About the Author

Angela Yuriko Smith is a two-time Bram Stoker Award–winning author, former president of the Horror Writers Association, and publisher of *Space and Time*. As a publishing consultant and coach, she helps writers build sustainable creative careers rooted in art, not arson. She writes *Authortunities* on Substack.

You can connect with me on:

- https://angelaysmith.com
- https://twitter.com/AngelaYSmith
- https://www.facebook.com/Angela.Yuriko.Smiths

Subscribe to my newsletter:

- https://authortunities.substack.com

Also by Angela Yuriko Smith

Angela Yuriko Smith is a third-generation Shimanchu/Ryukyuan-American, award-winning poet, author, and publisher with 20+ years of newspaper experience. Publisher of *Space & Time* magazine (est. 1966), a two-time Bram Stoker Awards® Winner, and an HWA Mentor of the Year, she shares *Authortunities*, a free weekly calendar of author opportunities at authortunit ies.substack.com.

Tortured Willows: Bent. Bowed. Unbroken.
THE BRAM STOKER AWARD® WINNER FOR SUPERIOR ACHIEVEMENT IN POETRY 2021

The willow is femininity, desire, death. Rebirth. With its ability to grow from a single broken branch, it is the living embodiment of immortality. It is the yin that wards off malevolent spirits. It is both revered and shunned.

In *Tortured Willows*, four Southeast Asian women writers of horror expand on the exploration of otherness begun with the Bram Stoker Award-winning anthology *Black Cranes: Tales of Unquiet Women*.

Like the willow, women have bent and bowed under the expectations and duty heaped upon them. Like the willow, they endure and refuse to break.

Unquiet Spirits: Essays by Asian Women in Horror
A BRAM STOKER AWARD® FINALIST FOR SUPERIOR ACHIEVEMENT IN NONFICTION 2023

From hungry ghosts, vampiric babies, and shapeshifting fox spirits to the avenging White Lady of urban legend, for generations, Asian women's roles have been shaped and defined through myth and story. In Unquiet Spirits, Asian writers of horror reflect on the impact of superstition, spirits, and the supernatural in this unique collection of 21 personal essays exploring themes of otherness, identity, expectation, duty, and loss, and leading, ultimately, to understanding and empowerment.

Bitter Suites
A BRAM STOKER AWARD® FINALIST FOR SUPERIOR ACHIEVEMENT IN LONG FICTION 2018

Book a stay at the Bitter Suites, a hotel that specializes in renewable death experiences. Whether you schedule your demise as therapy, to bond with a loved one or for pure recreation, your death is sure to give you a new lease on life. Renewable death is always beneficial… at least to someone.